DUELING PICKET FENCES

by

J. A. Elaine

authorHOUSE®

AuthorHouse™
1663 Liberty Drive, Suite 200
Bloomington, IN 47403
www.authorhouse.com
Phone: 1-800-839-8640

First published by AuthorHouse 3/20/2008

ISBN: 978-1-4343-4982-8 (sc)

Printed in the United States of America
Bloomington, Indiana

This book is printed on acid-free paper.

While the colonial town of Old Wethersfield was settled in 1634 and does currently exist, Windslow Street is a creation of this author. Given characters, names, and incidents are purely fictitious and any resemblance to actual events is coincidental.

Dedication

To dear Fran, whose friendship and support I treasure.

For my sweet daughter, Lauren; without your encouraging smile and affirming nod, this story would have been left unfinished.

To my wonderful husband, who has been there to champion my many adventures, but I am most grateful that he has yet to read this.

Most of all, I thank God for the peace of mind to complete this novel.

Prologue

October 28, 1977
Morning

They were an awesome sight. The trio of men appeared ready for a night of Halloween fright and frolic, but they were preparing for bigger pumpkins than that. In the cluttered basement, they gathered around the single light bulb, which swayed tentatively on its frayed cord. The yellowish glare surrounded the men like a superpower aura seen on comic book covers. The Dick Tracy boldness of color was clearly evidenced in each costume. Hank, the taller of the three and quite well built, was fastening a belt around a streamlined midriff, which brought together the layered guise of the infamous Batman. Standing close to the full mirror that leaned precariously on a mahogany wardrobe, he adjusted his mask and pushed back some unruly gray hairs. Then there was Joe. He had perched himself on a pile of oak crates and was struggling to pull on the thick tights, resembling a fat lady on television commercials. He cursed and groaned as he stuffed himself into the snug, polyester, red and blue suit, decorated with the lines for Spiderman, lines that girdled his expanding beer belly. The third fellow, Pete, the youngest, the shortest, and, by far, the most energized of the three, swiftly pulled on his superhero costume. Once blue tights met the red chest and flowing cape, the man impishly smiled and thrust up his arms in classic Olympian style, displaying well-chiseled muscles. He was Superman, and any passerby would have probably guessed him to be the real McCoy—that is, with the exception of the mask covering his carrot-colored hair.

At last they were ready. Hank, Joe, and Pete were transformed into other personalities, dedicated to a mission not to champion humanity but to promote themselves. Their costumes mirrored their base natures quite adequately. Clad in layers of black, Hank was shrouded in mystery—the enormity of his vile ways hidden. Joe was ensnarled in the many webs he had cast and woven so tightly. And Pete, dressed as a hero to save the day, was only out to save himself. He was out to pilfer the pockets of the rich and jam his own. Each critically inspected the outfit of the others, checking for any fault, pulling at a strand of material. Since the costuming was hand-tailored by Joe's wife, supposedly for a fright-night party, it had been rushed to its deadline. There were even stray common pins to pick out, which they carelessly tossed about Hank's flea-market cellar. Then each threw on muddied sneakers and ill-fitting trench coats, paying no attention to the break in coordination. Hank pulled up his sleeve and, realizing the time, hollered marching orders. In moments, the terrible three were ready to move on their adventure.

The brownstone building stood elegant and stately despite the loosening mortar and worn corners. The heavy rains of the evening before had dampened the structure so that a portion of brick and ivy had soaked in the moisture. A heavy drizzle continued to fall from a sky that portrayed a painter's hand of Payne's gray. Clad in raincoats, business stripes, and dark leather shoes, people rushed into the heavy glass doors of the regal edifice. The rusting Chevy met the curb quietly and efficiently. Hank pulled out the keys, puffing hard on his Borkim-Riff-filled pipe. The pungent aroma filled the interior of the car like a heavy cloud, causing Joe to cough and sputter. But Hank and Pete spent a long moment eyeing their cache: the New England National Bank.

It was a few minutes before ten thirty, so they had to wait. Hank had wanted it that way. He had frequented the bank in the mornings and found that there was a line at opening time that continued for a little over an hour. Then there was a lull in the activity, which would grant them access to healthy bank tills. Hank was not precise in most ways, but in this case, it had to be ten thirty or else. They also needed to keep a lucky charm of sorts with them. For Hank, it was his first ticket stub to a gangster movie. Joe took a Babe Ruth baseball card. The famous player was his hero because, in a single day, the Babe had broken two records: one for homeruns and the other for strikes. Joe secured the card to the side of his ankle, underneath his thick sock. Pete balked at this directive, refusing to take anything. He thought Hank was too superstitious, that he had listened to too many sleuth shows or thumbed through too many comic books. So ten thirty it was, and they had all finally agreed to it. Hank sat staring at his two watches: one on his wrist and the other grasped in his hand, a spare that he always kept in his glove compartment. Pete stared at the building as if trying to mesmerize a cougar with his Superman skill while Joe squirmed in his Spiderman suit, itching irritated skin and pulling at the tight fabric. Hank eased himself from the driver's seat, pointed to his watch, and waved Pete and Joe from the dingy car. Pete sprang from the back seat and attempted to remove his raincoat, but Hank motioned him to stop, so he re-zipped his outer coat and climbed out of the car. But Joe refused to move.

Hank gave Joe his vilest evil eye. "Get the hell out of the car!"

Joe remained as he was. He stroked his chin with two fingers and contorted his face as if he were sucking lemons.

Hank then spewed intense vulgarities as he waved his fists at Joe.

"You just try to make me, you rotten son of ..." said Joe as he quickly ducked his head. He positioned himself on the passenger seat as if tacked down there by those extra common pins. Pete nudged Hank and put his index finger to his mouth, strongly indicating the universal quiet sign. In a swift movement, Pete attempted to yank Joe from the car. But he was a moment too late. Joe quickly responded by repelling Pete with a keen kick to the groin. As the Superman hero fell awkwardly from the car, Joe slammed the door and the locks shut. A wiry Charlie Brown smile filled his face from ear to ear. Clearly Joe had outsmarted the cleverest of foxes, and now he had the den to himself—at least for a few minutes. Pete stood at the rear of the vintage vehicle, and with one hand, he steadied himself; with the other, he soothed his lower abdominal muscles. Recovery time was swift as Pete stood before Hank, square and tall—all five feet of him. Hints of his red cape edged about the hem of his raincoat. Superman was definitely ready to make an appearance. Hank's eyes enlarged and he pulled on his moustache. Pete moved towards the passenger seat, but in a flash, Hank was between him and the car. Pete was ready to show Joe some of his prized jabs and uppercuts he had perfected in prison. Angry utterances were silenced as Hank drew his arm around Pete, physically dissuading him from his effort. Hank anchored his gaze to the brownstone across the street and beckoned Pete to do so as well. Then, as if a trainer had blown the whistle, they marched across the street. Pete's face was chiseled in determination, his jaw tucked in and ready, while Hank's steel gray eyes danced in anticipation of what was to come, with or without Joe.

Joe watched as the two comrades in crime threw their raincoats into the bushes and entered the bank. They had decided to equal the tables of injustice and take back from the rich and cushion their calloused-hand lifestyle. He tugged at the Spiderman attire that he had managed to squirm into and couldn't wait to cast off. The hues of brick red and dark blue of the suit fit his dark mood; he was so agitated with Hank and Pete that he felt more like a villain than a superhero. Maybe, just maybe, he would turn those two hoodlums in and collect the reward money. They certainly would have it coming to them.

All these years, Hank would boss him around and get away with it. Like the time Hank stole some of his best cows and said they were rightfully his since they had wandered into his field and had been grazing. When he had confronted Hank, all he got was a wheelbarrow of excuses and a lot of blame put in his corner. It was, "Joe, you should have been watching your stock. Joe, you should have been mending your fences. Joe, you're a horrible farmer." Joe could sense his heart rate quickening as a surge of hatred filled his veins. His hands trembled, and the early breakfast of greasy bacon and runny eggs threatened to lurch from his innards. It was time to go. Should he just drive Hank's old jalopy and leave those two stranded without any get-away car? It would certainly serve them right. But what if the timing was all wrong and they found him in the car and connected him as an accomplice? That would be horrible for him. He would have a lot of explaining to do, especially to his wife Lena and their two kids. Why, he had gotten involved in all this to make life easier for them, not more difficult. He had not wanted to implicate them in any way, so it was for the best that he pulled out now. After all, he had his family to think about. Joe glanced over at the bank, which remained stately and quiet under the heavy drizzle. He pulled his charcoal raincoat about himself and stepped from the car into the damp air. Glancing in all directions, he headed towards the county store and the woodsy trail beyond.

Chapter One

Twenty years later
February 6, 1997

MONDAY EVENING

She just couldn't help herself. The more they did it, the more she wanted to do it. She was driven and she knew it. It wasn't about the prize anymore ... maybe it never was. But it was about that fantastic roller coaster high, the incredible twists and turns.

"Bette, come on. I can't wait all day! What did we clear?" asked Darcy sharply, her foot pushing the pedal so that the rusty Mustang surged forward. With her free right hand, she tossed their glittery but frayed Mardi Gras masks, which they had lifted years before in New Orleans, into the back seat. Then she took the hand pistol from her pocket and placed it in Bette's lap. "Just stick that in the glove compartment and then tell me."

"Hold on a minute." Bette yanked the handle and eased the gun into the small space. She took her key and secured the compartment and tossed it towards her pocketbook. She didn't realize she had missed and that the key had fallen and wedged itself in the deep well under the seat. "Um, let's see," said Bette as she emptied the contents of the paper bag into her lap. With the expectation of a small child on Christmas morn, Bette filtered and sifted through the items.

"Well?" said Darcy as she glanced over at her friend and then to the rearview mirror. All clear. Her shoulders arched as she took a deep breath and smoothed strands of her shoulder-length tresses. The last few minutes, she had felt the rush of a deep-sea diver discovering Atlantis. She loved every minute of it.

Bette had wasted no time. In moments, she had everything in itemized piles on her lap. "It looks like we got $865 and change, three checks, credit cards, an ID card, several Dreamy Decadent chocolate bars, and thirteen jelly beans," Bette said as she hastily unwrapped a crispy bar and shoved it into her mouth.

"Jelly beans!"

"Yeah, I think that guy behind the counter was munching on this candy when we made our surprise visit."

Darcy's smile widened. "Like someone I know. Bette you had better take it easy on the chocolate or they will be calling us the Mardi Gras Sweeties." She glanced over at her friend's lap. "The catch was decent, but not great; but added to the rest, it will do. We'll dump the checks. Hmm … perhaps a bit of shopping is in order."

"Why do we always dump the checks? I've read somewhere that if you soak the checks in a certain household chemical, the ink will come out. You just have to be careful to cover the signature with tape so the check can be reused. Do you want to try it?"

Darcy shrugged. "It's messy. I'm just not interested in doing that right now."

"Gosh, some of these checks have lots of information on them: phone numbers, full addresses, and even Social Security numbers. I understand you could easily rob people with stuff like that. We could invest in a computer and work from home so we wouldn't have to go out so much. Darcy, I've read that one day everyone will own a computer and that stealing like this will be real easy."

"There's no fun in that," said Darcy as she squirmed in her seat. "You know that I've become an adrenaline junkie with all our capers. Of course, you know that you've been my best bet, and your name being Bette has been a lucky charm for me."

"Yeah, always with the sweet talk. But if we try something different, maybe we can stay in one place and get a life and perhaps even meet some guys."

Darcy's left eyebrow arched in opposition. "Now why would you want to go and do that and break up our wonderful track record? And who needs guys? You know that we work well together."

"It's just that we're always out there, constantly putting ourselves in danger. Even with this last job at the mart …"

"What, that Marty's Complete? Hey, we protected ourselves by casing that place so we realized we had cameras to smash!"

"Yeah, yeah, I know. I would just like to be more hidden; we've been on the front lines forever."

"Well. I'll think about it. But for right now, can we just get rid of the checks?"

Bette sighed in resignation. "Okay, I'll dump them, but really think about it for the next time, okay? Right now, I think we should leave this town and that last store way behind us."

"Agreed," said Darcy as she maneuvered the vehicle onto a ramp leading to parts north. The sharp turn caused a rockslide of checks and cash. Darcy grasped at the falling loot and gasped, "What the hell is this!"

Darcy caught the flying charge card and license.

"Stop the stupid stunts, you idiot," shouted Bette, her aquamarine eyes wide and unblinking. "We're going to get into an accident. Maybe your antics will even get us some police attention."

Darcy turned the cards over in her hand and stared hard. "You see it, don't you?"

"I do, but this is incredible. I can't believe it."

"Well, what do you think? Quite a goldmine, isn't it?"

"I'd say." Bette continued to stare at the photograph. "You know, with the right shaping of my hair, a bit of lightened color to make it a bit more blond, and a little makeover, I could be her."

"Exactly what I was thinking, Bette. We're going to have some fun with this one, especially if we dye that dirty blonde hair of yours and give you a little touch of makeup," said Darcy. She winked playfully at Bette as she pulled a strand of her friend's hair.

"Hey, you're not such hot stuff yourself. Why, you've never even touched a bottle of foundation or tried a lip color, and you haven't washed that head of yours in … I can't remember!"

"I haven't had time, that's all," rationalized Darcy, her gray eyes narrowed so that she resembled an evil cartoon character. "And this is about you, not me!" She pulled her hair forward so that it cascaded over her tattered jean jacket and sectioned off her face like a set of stage curtains.

With a sharp turn, Darcy angled the car towards a small town in Connecticut, to that infamous place where she had spent a lot of time as a kid, Windslow Street. A place where, long ago, she had been court-ordered to live with her aunt and uncle. The rearing she experienced there was far from the rural farmland her uncle's house sat on. She was indebted to him; she had been in trouble and he had bailed her out, although he had not been a squeaky-clean role model. In fact, she suspected many of his involvements were cloaking sinister dealings. But she had liked it that way. She had been taught wayward manners that fell beneath the line of the law. Darcy chuckled. There was a day long ago when, on a shopping spree at the strip mall, she and her uncle took home more than they presented at the counter. And they got away with it, scot-free. Good old Uncle Hank. She would like to see how he was doing and chill out for a while. The small town called Wethersfield and the road called Windslow would be just to her liking.

"Hey, I thought we were going farther than this. This little town, what was it called— Wethersfield—is not far enough away from that mart. Don't you think …?"

"Shut up! This is far enough. I have an uncle here who will be able to help us."

"Help us? We haven't needed anyone before."

"Will you please shut up? This will work fine; you'll see." Darcy expertly cut across three lanes to access the turnpike. Several cars blared their horns noisily at her Nascar antics.

"Darcy, what the heck? Are you trying to get us killed?"

"No, just tying to set us in the right direction, and when do you ever complain about my driving? I can drive blindfolded and never get in an accident!"

"You're a crazy show-off who has had a lucky leprechaun by her side, but one day things will change and I hope I'm not sitting here."

Darcy exaggerated a yawn and stretched her arms one at a time. "Bette, you worry too much."

"Yeah, just look at you. You're dead tired and so am I. It's after twelve, and I'm ready for bed. Your uncle is really going to want to see us in the middle of the night."

Darcy looked over at her accomplice and pursed her lips. "Maybe you're right. It's kind of late, and I remember that Uncle Hank was more vigilant at night." Darcy turned into a vacant church parking lot and drove to an obscure corner. She cut the engine. Snowflakes landed heavily on the windshield.

"We are stopping here, in this abandoned place? Why can't we just find a motel for the night so we can get a warm shower and watch a little TV?" Bette glared at Darcy.

"Because I said so. Besides, why spend all our money on a stupid room when I have blankets in the back?" Darcy reached over the seat and pulled out two coarse army blankets and tossed one at Bette. "Here, there are even a couple bags of potato chips to munch on."

Bette shrugged and directed her stare at Darcy. "I'm amazed how it's always your decision; mine is like slimy banana peels." She pushed her seat back and wrapped herself in the dank-smelling blanket.

"Hey, Bette, what's that on your wrist?"

"Nothing."

"But I've never seen it before," said Darcy, leaning over to investigate.

"Here; look! Now are you happy? It's just a charm bracelet I got on that back desk with the money and all. I found it, and I'm going to keep it!"

"So keep it. I certainly don't want it. You like candy, you like jewelry, what will be next?" Darcy gazed down at Bette, who had settled in and was either ignoring her or had nodded out. She decided to do the same as she curled her hand, hammered all the sticky car locks, and tossed a blanket into the driver's seat.

Chapter Two
TUESDAY

Hank impatiently watched the blackened, grease-stained pot as he edged the temperature knob so that the blue flames licked at it. He was edgy as usual. But morning coffee came before anything else. Without it, he was an incorrigible bear. He was nicknamed Grizzly Adams. Hank gazed at his reflection in the clear silver of the aluminum pan and figured them right. He looked the part. The oily locks of his graying hair fell about his ears, and his beard ached for a pair of decent trimmers. Dried mud crusted his eyebrows, earned by wood-chopping the day before. His eyes were usually gray, but when he became agitated, they would become a deep indigo. Hank's attire was comfortable blue jean stuff, with a filthy undershirt and ragged red plaid overshirt. Folks said he looked like he slept in his clothes, and that part they got right; he hadn't changed since sometime last week. And bathing. He hadn't cared for that in a long, long time.

The water had reached its boiling peak and was hopping out of the pan. Hank scooped a heaping amount of coffee grounds and threw them between the rolling rapids. He watched eagerly as the pot became an angry, sloppy brew. He grabbed a handful of eggshells that he had crushed, maybe last week, and scattered them into the makeshift coffee maker. Then just as his father had done, he picked up the pot and poured the vicious mixture into a rusty sieve. Taking his favorite mug, which stated, in darkened letters, "Live Big or Die," he poured the potent concoction. He brought the cup up to his nose and took a long sniff. The he gulped at it. Once again, he seared his throat, but he didn't care. He was thick-skinned; he could take it.

Through the knee-high piles of saved newspaper, Hank edged over to the window with his cup. Daybreak had created a lovely golden glimmer upon the virgin snow about him. It reminded Hank of old times, times when the backyard extended for miles. The abundant acreage lent fun and frolic to him and his younger brothers, as they enjoyed a sled ride or an all-out snowball fight. He could almost see the frozen faces and hear the high-pitched squeals of delight. But then his brothers died. It was a very hard blow; Hank took it personally. They had taken the easy way out and left him responsible for caring for his demanding, opprobrious father. But one day, an accident on the broken-down tractor ended that scene. Things got better after that. He acquired the dairy farm and married a woman, a wonderful lady. She was one of a kind, the sort who would do anything for anyone, although she had her faults. A tight grimace cracked his dry lips.

"Yep," he thought aloud as he puffed on his pipe, "she even changed me." While dairy farmers always seemed to be picking manure out of their fingernails, she had helped to clean up his disposition. He had been kinder back then. But she had her faults. She had nagged too much and at times she was a royal pain in the ass.

"What the hell?" Putting down his favorite pipe, he threw on his tattered parka and boots, and rushed out the door. He rolled a quick snowball and aimed it directly before him. The launched snow crashed the maroon woolen cap of one of the neighborhood kids.

"Get out! This is not your property. This is mine! You get one warning or I'll get my gun!" Hank bellowed.

The boys paused, disbelieving. A second snowball was launched. The boys wasted no time slipping and sliding out of there. He had showed them. Hank's upper lip twitched nervously; the wrinkles in his forehead deepened. He looked around. Houses, houses everywhere. The mountain was gone. The makeshift ice ring, gone. The dairy farm was gone. His lovely wife was gone as well. He had sold it all, and all he had left were bills and regrets. It had left him old and vengeful.

He turned his head towards the lopsided, weathered, brick-colored barn. Though muffled, he could hear a motor idling rough, as if the engine had caught a cold. Who could that be? Trudging quickly through the drifts of snow, Hank noted the twirl of the exhaust and the metallic red against the piled snow banks.

"What the hell are you doing by my barn? Who are you crazy people? Stay away from me!" Hank shouted as he approached the car with his arms flailing about him.

Darcy and Bette gazed in astonishment.

Bette's mouth hung agape.

Darcy nervously scratched her ear.

Who was this maniac, anyway? Now Darcy had known her uncle to be quite ornery and a bit eccentric. And she knew a thing or too about danger. But this guy had fallen off the edge.

"Let's get out of here!" said Bette as she roughly nudged her friend in the ribs.

"Ouch! Why did you do that?"

"You're not moving. I say we find somewhere else to go!"

The key hastily went into the ignition as an elbow pounded the side window, attempting to shatter it. Unsuccessful, Hank quickly surveyed the area and noted a rusted shovel perched near a snow bank. He hoisted the farm tool toward the car window. Darcy gasped and quickly rolled down the window. "Please don't," she pleaded. A weathered hand, full of age spots that belied the man's strength, reached in and grabbed Darcy's leather coat collar.

"Who are you?" Hank shouted, his demeanor extremely violent. Darcy pushed away the arm that carried a strong scent of tobacco. She could taste the sickening sweetness of blood in her mouth. She had bitten her tongue.

"What the hell are you doing, Uncle Hank! It's me. Can't you tell it's me, Darcy?"

Hank pulled his hand back in and peered into the window. Two traumatized faces stared back, pensive and scared.

It was a long moment.

Then the cracked lips smiled, and Hank remembered. Yes, he remembered. Darcy—son of a gun, Darcy.

"I guess you girls aren't just paying a friendly visit." Looking over on the other woman's lap, he noted some fresh Jackson and Grant bills. Indeed, they had been minding the store, two partners in crime. He liked that. He liked that a lot. "So you decided to finally pay your ol' Uncle Hank a visit."

Darcy and Bette nodded in unison.

"So are you two in need of a place to hide out?" Hank asked playfully. "Just like old times."

"Ah, well, I don't think so…" began Bette.

"You'd better believe it," said Darcy, eyeing her uncle resolutely.

"Well then, don't just sit there wasting gas; grab your stuff and come in for coffee," said Hank as he turned his heel and headed for the farmhouse. He then turned abruptly on his heeled boot. "On second thought, let's first get rid of this heap of rotting tin."

Darcy and Bette nodded and followed Uncle Hank into the garage.

Chapter Three

Joliana swiped the beads of sweat running from her woolen cap. Her toes were ice-capped but her head was being slowly steamed cooked. She hastily removed her woolen red cap. Her matted pageboy spilled out as she tousled her corn-colored hair to restore some life to it. Then she crammed the hat into her jacket pocket and studied the concrete steps she had just shoveled. She looked at her handiwork. Snake-like passages angled their way in the drifts of snow, marking clear passage. The walkways were nearly perfect, the piled snow evenly distributed, like the work of a newfangled snow blower. Joliana sighed and rubbed her lower back.

Almost done.

"Hey, Jo," yelled her father, "I hope you're finished out there!"

"Yea, yea, almost," said Joliana, "and I can't wait." She definitely was ready. Her arms felt limp and her stomach was a persistent rumble.

"Joliana, please hurry it on up!" demanded her father as he slammed the door.

No more endearments now. He called her by her full name, which he always did when he was really peeved. Joliana. What a name. Since grade school she had to endure the snickers and the strange looks she would get as teacher after teacher destroyed her name. But having a last name like Williard meant you sat in the back, a plus if you wanted to catnap but not so good if you were being singled out for something. She could still feel the twenty-five sets of eyes boring into her forehead. Her mother had always tried to console her with the fact that the name was a composite of the family tree: there was Jo for her father Joe, Lia for her mother Lenadora, and Ana for her grandmother Anna; and yes, there was Joli for her Uncle Jolly. Ah, the good old days.

Now her name had changed from Williard to Faracelli, and she was a grown woman with a family and children of her own to raise. But to her father, she was still Jo, or today, Joliana. Gosh, she couldn't wait to hang up her shovel and just head home. But she knew her father had other plans. Joliana stomped towards the old-fashioned bungalow.

"Well, well. It's about time," said her father as he slurped his sweetened coffee. "I was hoping you would get me a tuna sandwich."

"Yes, yes, just let me clean up." *Just who eats tuna in the morning?* she wondered. Her father did. He definitely had his ways and his own timing on things.

"Hurry up. I can't wait all day. My coffee will get cold."

"I'll get it," said Joliana in a cool tone. She wondered when her life had been rounded up by bandits, hogtied, and thrown into the smelly shed. When was she going to come out?

"What's the matter with you? Got an attitude! Well, you know I don't need that. Not with that good-for-nothing Staller family down the street. All they give me is trouble, you know the rotten son …"

"You want mayo and onion?" Joliana interjected.

"Both."

"And how about a bit of parsley?"

"I guess."

"Toasted or plain?"

Mr. Williard looked up from his mug and glowered at his daughter. "You're acting mighty stupid right now. You know how I like it. Just like your mom used to make it."

"Mom this and Mom that."

"What did you say?"

"Uh, nothing," said Joliana. But she knew. Ever since Mom had died years ago, her mother's ways and means had become immortalized. Her mother had done everything: dishes, laundry, even wood chopping. This all had created a horrific outcome: one very helpless man. She loved her dad but she definitely did not want to become her mom's carbon copy. She often wondered how she could be so self-sufficient and an extreme perfectionist while her father was the king of all slobs. But she knew that she took after her mother; Joliana was indeed a nurturer and could be awarded on Mother's Day. The many years since she died had dimmed her memory of certain things, but she would never forget her mother's open heart and warm embrace. Her mom had always been there to listen to the everyday calamites of her life with an intent gaze and a nod of affirmation. Indeed, she hoped she was doing as well with her own children.

Joliana shoved the plate before her dad. She had prayed for patience this morning, but she had no way near the tolerance of Job.

"Aren't you having one?"

"No."

"Well, in that case, could you pick up some groceries and throw in some laundry? That is, unless you don't mind that I do them my way, in the tub," asked her father rather impatiently.

Joliana nodded obediently and ran over to the dingy laundry room, which was attached to the side of the garage. As she pushed aside a sticky web, she made a promise to herself to return soon with a broom and rag. Joliana hastily piled a dark mix of her father's clothing into the rusty Maytag. Then she hastened into the kitchen and snatched the grocery list off the greasy tablecloth and squinted hard. It was always a challenge making sense of her father's second grade scribble. As she headed for the door, her dad quietly walked behind her and placed his hand on her shoulder.

"You know, Jo, I appreciate all you do around here."

Yes, I know." Joliana sighed. He was back to using her sobriquet.

"And you know with your mother not here, and with this big house and all, that I need you."

"Yeah."

"Well, just remember that I'm here for you," he said endearingly as he pinched her cheek.

"I know, Dad," said Joliana as she eyed her father. Somehow he always knew when to ladle on the smooth talk.

"Well, see you later." Joe paused and scratched his head. "Well, one more thing before you go: could you clear the snow out from the garage and then bring out the garbage pails? And here's another list for some things at the hardware store." Joe smiled hopefully.

"Dad, you're really trying to build the Crossway Bridge in one day. I'll do my best to shovel and make a run to the hardware store, but the groceries might have to wait until tomorrow," said Joliana in an irritated voice. Gosh, her father always wanted things done yesterday, but she knew she cared for him, and she could tell by the thinning white hairs that he was getting older.

Joe shrugged. "Oh, one more thing: could you put a bowl of food and some water out for Boomer? Thanks. Well, I'm going to finish my tuna. Bye."

Joliana nodded but turned her head so that her father would not see her scrunch up her face like she was sucking lemons. On the porch, she filled both doggie bowls to the top and then glanced around the yard. Where was Boomer? She had found the chocolate Labrador at a nearby rescue.

He was perfect for her dad, very friendly as well as protective. And her dad loved him so much that he let Boomer have his freedom to wander about the neighborhood. So much for a guard dog. She then angled through the snowdrifts to the garage. She had better get working while the morning was still young, so she could cross a few items off her father's demanding list.

"Hey, Dad, when is Mom getting back?"

"Don't know. She went over to Grandpa's a while ago."

"What's she doing there now?" asked Karen in an irritated tone.

"I guess Grandpa's got her doing his usual: cleaning, shopping, cooking. She was even swinging a shovel a few minutes ago."

"I could have done that. I like shoveling new snow."

"I know, but Grandpa asked her, and you know how he gets very impatient."

"Hi, guys," interrupted Brad. "What's going on?"

Tony Faracelli looked up fondly at his teenage son and two daughters. "Just talking about Mom and Grandpa."

"It's always about Mom and Grandpa," added five-year-old Susie. "I want Mommy home."

"She'll be back in a few minutes. Prepare yourself a simple lunch today, like peanut butter and corn chips. And get moving. Even though last night's snow caused a late opening, you don't want to dawdle and miss that bus. And you too, young lady." Tony smiled playfully at Susie. "We'll have to de-ice the truck, just in case the bus doesn't show up, like last time."

"Okay," said Susie as she wrapped her arms around her dad's growing midriff.

"Hey, Dad, how come Grandpa can't do some things himself? He doesn't seem sick," said Brad.

"That's a good question," remarked Susie.

Tony shrugged. "Don't know, really. I guess it became a habit. He was so used to your grandma doing and doing that he forgot how."

"Yeah, or maybe he doesn't want to," said Karen.

"I agree, and he's still got a lot of energy left. In fact, I saw him have a hollering fit at Mr. Staller the other day. They were only a few feet from each other. They came close to having a good old-fashioned fight," said Brad.

Tony looked up from his cereal and newspaper, his left bushy eyebrow arched in concern. The two widowed old codgers were at it again. "What stopped them?" His bushy eyebrow arched curiously.

"Well, it happened in the parking lot of Don's Dairy Mart. I guess the place was too public," said Brad.

"Public my foot!" said their father. "That Mr. Staller is such a braggart; I can't see that stopping him."

"It's because he's got guns," Susie asserted in her delicate voice.

"Hah," Karen said. "It's because Grandpa's always been afraid of Mr. Staller!"

"And what for?" demanded Brad.

"I told you, because he's got guns," Susie said adamantly, stomping her foot.

Ignoring the comment, Tony pulled Susie over and placed the petite child on his knee.

"It's like this. Years and years ago, Mr. Staller claimed that one of his best milking cows wandered off into Grandpa's land and was feeding in his pasture.

"So?"

"Did the cow ever wander back to Mr. Staller?"

"Why did the cow leave?"

The perplexed, curious children fired their earnest inquiries at their dad, their breakfast toast and eggs becoming cold.

"Hold on; wait a minute here," said Tony, waving his hand to silence the interrogation.

"Now let me see. The cow just roamed away for no particular reason, and I don't believe Grandpa gave it back."

"Why not?" all three of the children said together.

"Well, he believed that since the cow was on his property, that it was his."

"He did what?"

"Like I said, he took the cow. It was in his yard, so Grandpa saw it as fair game."

"And how did the cow get out?" asked young Susie.

"Good question, Susie," said their jovial, red-cheeked father. "I think the cow was grazing in Mr. Staller's meadow field and somehow got through one of the broken fences."

"But, Dad, are you sure? I have never even heard of a meadow field. Where is that?" said Karen.

"It's gone," said Tony as a morsel of regret clung to his throat. "The thing is, Mr. Staller and Grandpa had both sold off most of the huge acreage of land they had farmed on."

"You mean where all these lawns are, it was farmland?" said Karen.

"Yes, with lots of chickens and pigs, a good amount of cows, and even a couple of horses. You know that your Mom grew up here, right across the street. She remembers having a load of chores to do,like milking cows, gathering eggs, and cleaning the barn. We should ask Mom to tell us more about her farm days. But right now, you all better throw on your coats and head out to school."

All three nodded.

"But why is it that Mom doesn't talk much about those days? I would like to know," said the curious thirteen-year-old Brad.

Tony looked over Susie's head and gazed out the kitchen bay window. "Something else I recall is that there was some problem with their deeds, a deed being an official paper that says who owns what. Grandpa thought that Mr. Staller cheated on the boundaries and, as a result, made a heck of a lot more money."

"So that's why there's been so much fighting over the years," said Brad, his cornflower eyes bright with insight.

"Yes, yes, and it will probably go on and on, especially since neighborhood disputes of this sort can get really nasty," and then he whispered, "and they can end violently." Tony grabbed a napkin and wiped milk from his mouth. He would never forget the argument of years past that had destroyed Lizzie's family, making her crazier than ever. The jingle of the wind chimes above the kitchen entry diverted their attention. Mom was home.

Joliana's aquamarine eyes twitched, and her peach-colored lips were pursed, resulting in deep furrows in her chin, definitely not her best side. She hastily removed her sodden boots and gloves.

"Mom's home!" said the children as they clamored about, attempting to get her attention.

"Not for long. I just wanted to change out of these wet things before I set out to run some errands for the marts and for Grandpa. And you kids better get your coats on. The bus will be here soon!" Joliana was now attempting to pull off her damp socks.

"Hey, Jo, with the late opening, the kids and I had an interesting talk about things. I'll have to tell you later. But right now, since you're headed out, could you take the kids to school? That is, if the darn bus doesn't show. It's already late! Hey, I'll even do the dishes!" As Tony made his offering, his eyes twinkled mischievously.

"Yeah, that will work," said Joliana as she zipped her boots. "I can make a full circle: drop the kids, get Grandpa's stuff, and hopefully get to the three marts to make a drop at the bank."

"Well, be careful. See you at supper," said Tony as he gave Joliana a quick kiss on her still-frozen cheek. In moments, the house cleared of the morning banter, and Tony turned to the sink to make good on his promise, wondering how Joliana kept up with all these demands.

The phone's shrill call interrupted his thoughts.

"Hello."

"Tony, this is Marty. I have some bad news. The mart was robbed last night, late, right before closing. They got a full load of …"

"What? We were robbed last night and you tell me now? What is your problem? May I remind you that we all should work together …"

"Now, Tony, don't start in on your lecture of how you and your nephew are co-owners in this business. I know, I know. I thought I could handle it. But there are a couple of problems that I could use your help on."

"I should say so! I know this business. Before I married Joliana, my family ran a hardware store. And my father told me about these thieves …"

"Tony, I can't talk now, but I could sure use your help here," said Marty firmly.

There was a brief pause as Tony breathed audibly into the phone and replied, "I'll be there as soon as possible." With that, he hung up his kitchen towel and headed out the door.

Chapter Four

Joliana Faracelli had not always been married with three children. She had been a Willard daughter much longer, a young girl with so many dreams. She loved history and would surround herself with many a novel concerning the Revolutionary War and early Colonial life. And why not? She was raised in an ancient town in Connecticut, a quaint place called Wethersfield, established in 1634. She loved visiting the vintage village called Old Wethersfield, and she did so over and over again. She would ride her bike with ease through the old town, enjoying the layout of the homes and the sense of early Colonial lifestyle. Part of her habitual tour would be to visit the Webb house for the admission of a shiny quarter. After a while, the guides became so used to her visitation that they let her freely roam the house. Joliana enjoyed this freedom. She would spend time in the chamber where George Washington had slept, appreciating the flocked wallpaper, which she would select in later years for her own home. Her favorite spots were the slave quarters and the kitchen. She envisioned most of the daily life happening here and could almost smell the comfort food being prepared. Indeed, sometimes she thought she could feel the presence of the Webb family: their comings and goings, their joys and sadness. This was perhaps all due to a clever imagination and wishful hopes to be a historian—until she heard about the strange happenings in these colonial homes, especially for those people who either bought or rented. Such things like footsteps creaking on stairs, rearrangement of furniture, sudden icy spots in a relatively warm room. These kinds of things intrigued her as well as spooked her silly. But all that strange stuff didn't deter her from wanting to live in one of these old houses, perhaps when she either got married or had enough money of her own. There was one colonial in particular, a stately white clapboard with black shutters, bearing the placard of prior ownership by an early American family. It was rumored that odd things happened in that house, which would account for the frequent turnover, but to Joliana, this talk only added to her desire and eventual occupancy. Besides, it was across the street from her childhood home, making it convenient to drop by whenever she wanted.

Joliana's visit wasn't complete until she rode her bike down to the cove. With her sunflower-colored hair dancing in the wind, she would pedal as fast as she could to the weathered barn that was positioned near the water. Sometimes the wooden structure would be at water's edge if there had been much storming. But today was idyllic, with the waves cresting so evenly it was hypnotic. The lovely crystal color reflected in her turquoise eyes. The sun was bold and warm, and Joliana would often rest a bit on a shady patch of grass. She would angle her freckled face to the sky and think about everything and nothing.

Joliana had often hoped that her future would bring work as a historian. Yet when it came to college, she didn't have the resources or the drive to complete all those years. Instead, she opted for nursing, a vocation that had also fascinated her as she studied recent war epics and such notables as Clara Barton. So nursing school it was. Initially, she had done fine; her academics were stellar, but the practicum eluded her. When she was involved in hands-on testing, it had to be perfect, everything just so. No one in her class had seen such flawless behavior, especially her professor. She was the lovely blue diamond in the rough. Joliana would complete a task, evaluating each step, and even though it was acceptable, she would repeat it again and again. Indeed, compared to her, a tortoise would have received a road race award. Joliana was obstinate. She argued her case to her superiors, that she was careful in her work and extremely accurate. Didn't that count for something? Apparently not. They wanted quantity and quality in balanced amounts and thought she would never cut it on a nursing floor.

So Joliana tried to speed up and compete with her classmates. Her efforts backfired like a faulty pistol. Both her grades and clinical skills plummeted, and she found her health deteriorating. She had shortness of breath, her heart rate accelerated, she sweated through her clothing, and her hands acquired a terrible tremble. So the nursing stint came to an end.

But right before her departure, she met Tony. He had been attending the same college, just in another section that accommodated business administration. Their buildings were located so far apart, it was a miracle that they met at all. But she had been praying to meet a decent young man, one who was also faithful in his prayers as well as committed to finding his place in the world of work. He was someone who was down to earth and would like to do some of the fun things she liked to do, such as hiking and visiting historic sites.

So one day, Joliana stopped by the student center to grab a sandwich and coffee. She was in one of her anxious modes, and as she set up her table to eat, she didn't notice that Tony was trying to sit at the same table. In her clumsy greeting, she spilled her hot brew in his lap. Not exactly the most romantic way to begin a relationship. However, it had become stellar ever since. In just a few weeks, she was wearing a wonderful tear-shaped diamond ring, with plans to walk down that church aisle. She quickly became a mother, with two daughters and a son sandwiched between. They bought a lovely home across the street from her folks, the same one she had admired as a kid. Needless to say, she had ample opportunity to utilize her nursing skills and historian directives right at home.

Joliana had been satisfied with her family and all her many functions, until recently. Lately, she was not content with things. She had poured all her energies into her home, which was resplendent with decorative antique lace positioned just so. Gourmet meals were prepared with the special touch of home-grown vegetables and herbs, and she had a thumb in every one of her children's activities. Then there were the three dairy marts, Don's Dairy, The Marty Complete, and Dairy Plus, that were owned jointly between her father, husband, and brother-in-law. Her part was to assist in management and finances. Her drive for perfection and strict organization made this a good match most of the time, when her patience wasn't tried. But there were many times when factoring other things, such as employees, into the mix caused situations to get out of hand. People. These difficult personalities were making her life unsettling, and her father topped them all. It always seemed that everyone was tugging at her shirt sleeves, saying, "Do this and do that." When would there ever be time for her? Maybe never. Not with kids, household obligations, and the dairy mart family business. But it was not all bad. Being Mrs. Faracelli was not always a breathtaking, cloudless day, but she knew she loved her husband and kids and had a wonderful life. It just needed a bit of fresh jalapeño pepper to spice it up.

Joliana readied herself to head out, capping her head with her favorite woolen hat, securing a few runaway blonde hairs. She didn't realize that her life was just about to be kicked up a gear to a place that would leave her breathless.

Chapter Five

Geraldine Pryor let the antique lace fall delicately from her fingertips and hastily ascended to the second level of the three-story bungalow. She settled her girth into her favorite Hitchcock-designed rocker and drew closer to the left-side window, which held a pivotal view in the charming widow's peak. How she loved it up here. She could rock and rock and gaze for miles, taking in the comings and goings of the neighborhood.

"Oh my, what is that?" said Geraldine as she inched closer to the window, tucking a long gray wisp into her tight hair bun. She adjusted her thin-framed glasses on her wide nose to accommodate the set of fine binoculars. Just like always, Hank Staller was up to something strange. That was his usual, but today her interest was definitely piqued.

Geraldine inched the window open a good inch or so. The frosty air wasted no time chilling her cheek. But she didn't care.

"Okay, ladies, let's do this right—the first time," demanded Hank. "Let's get all the car parts out of that side of the garage and place them in the shed."

"All right, all right, we're going as fast as we can," said Bette.

"No, you're not. Let's move it. This red jalopy is far too visible."

"Well, who's gonna see us? It's a quiet county street and everyone is working," said Darcy impatiently.

"Yeah, yeah, that's what you think, but I know the trees have eyes."

"What?" Bette and Darcy asked simultaneously.

"Yeah, you heard me. Believe it, after all these years, I know. People see. People talk."

"I figure we have something to hide, but Hank, what do you have to worry about?" said Bette.

"None of your business," Hank muttered angrily.

The pace picked up as Darcy and Bette hastily moved items—a lawnmower, automotive tools, pieces of a bygone carburetor. Then Bette scooped the keys from Darcy's pocket and positioned their well-worn wheels into the snug garage.

Darcy threw the gray backpack over her shoulder and gingerly grasped the handle of the antique briefcase.

Geraldine inched forward to the panes so that the rims of the binoculars were turning. Something green hung from the side of the briefcase. Then, as the boots hastened, the green fell, making a sort of bread-crumble, Hansel and Gretel walkway. Geraldine squinted. She could swear it was currency. But she couldn't be sure.

Geraldine had to find out. Throwing on her winter jacket, she hurried downstairs to the front door and grabbed the handle.

Then she paused.

Geraldine wanted to, but she just couldn't. Her lovely lavender eyes misted over as her hand fell limp from the doorknob. She couldn't, because she had not left her house in twenty years.

Bette rubbed her hands over the peeling gray radiator as it gurgled and spit out its warmth.

"What I could go for is some real hot chocolate!" she said hopefully.

"Yeah, Uncle Hank, instead of that mud you call coffee," added Darcy as she shook the pan laden with heavy coffee grounds.

"You'll get some good eats once you show me what's in the case," demanded Hank.

Darcy's hand tightened about the handles of the dilapidated case. "Don't know what you mean, Uncle."

"Don't play all sweet to me, Darcy. Let's be perfectly honest here; I've haven't seen you in years. Why, I hardly recognized you when you rudely barged in. And your father, well, you probably know we weren't exactly friends and I blew off his funeral."

"Now wait a minute, Uncle Hank. I did call you, but you never returned my calls," said Darcy.

"And I never will."

"C'mon, lighten up, Uncle Hank; you're awfully intense."

"Me, intense!" Hank turned to the girls. He stood squarely in front of Darcy and forced his indigo eyes wide. "You should talk! I've heard things about you. You've got a reputation, I know. And this sidekick of yours, Bette is it? Well she's good for a job or two, until she slips up."

Showing definite discoloration due to a steady flow of chocolate and coffee, Bette's large mouth hung open wide, showing her lack of dental help.

Darcy poised her tall body so she looked taller and countered her uncle's ugly stare with a her strongest scowl.

"So you want a fight, do you," Darcy said angrily.

"Not really. I just want to see what's in the case."

"Well, you don't treat a fellow Staller like that. I want respect," said Darcy tensely.

"Ha … respect. I don't think so," said Hank.

Then an arm catapulted towards Hank's cheek.

Hank ducked.

Darcy lost her footing and fell into the lumpy pile of newspapers near the kitchen chair.

The infamous attaché hit the linoleum.

Its contents emptied.

An astonished hush hung in the air.

"Damn," said Hank.

"For crying out loud," said Bette.

"It's not what you think," said Darcy as she hastily fell to her knees, retrieving the green bills.

"Yes, yes, pick it all up, and we'll count it," said Hank.

"But it isn't that much," hedged Darcy.

"It's enough proof of your Bonnie and Clyde life."

"What will you do? You won't turn us in?" said Bette.

"Hardly," said Hank. "In fact, it seems to me that since you came to hide out for a while that we could make some plans …"

"Plans?" said both girls.

"Yeah," said Hank as he tossed a coffee mug towards Bette.

"Here, knock yourself out," said Hank as he stooped to pluck up some bills and the two cards.

Bette obediently sauntered over to the stove to boil more water for coffee and caught a glimpse of something moving outside the window. She moved closer.

"Uncle Hank—or should I call you that—who is outside in the backyard?"

Hank threw the bills in a pile on the soiled checkered tablecloth and stepped over to Bette's side.

"That crazy Owens lady? What is she doing?"

"Owens … do you mean sweet Lizzie?" asked Darcy innocently.

"Yeah, sweet as arsenic. Remember what I told you about neighbors having eyes and ears? Well, what—she is picking up something! Why, I think she has a handful of bills! I'm going to give her a piece of my mind," said Hank as he headed towards the door.

Darcy intercepted his departure and flung her arm out.

"Don't go."

"Get out of my way or you'll be sorry."

"No."

"You don't know what you're doing here."

"I think I do," said Darcy obstinately. "If you go all wild, then that woman will really think something's going on."

Hank halted. The inky depth of Hank's eyes seemed to brighten. Darcy was right.

He had to calm down.

Through the soiled, thin curtains, all three studied the woman. They froze in place like a professional mime team. What was she doing? With the green bills hanging from her pockets, Lizzie Owens was frantically looking for more. She had left the cleared walk and was stomping through the snowdrifts in her slippers, light blue flannel nightgown, and sweater. Her movements were jerky, and what they could see of her face showed that strange smile was there. Scary, it was. Lizzie's sloppily reddened lips were set in a rigid grimace that angled up into an odd grin, like those of evil circus clowns. And those huge sunglasses, always there, always perched a bit off center. But Lizzie was not evil, just strange and eccentric.

"What's she up to?" said Darcy.

"No good, I'll tell you," said Hank.

"Look, I think she's coming this way. She's going to knock any minute!" said Bette.

"Damn!" yelled Hank.

"No, wait, she's turned. I think she changed her mind," interjected Darcy.

"She had better leave, or I'll go out there and bodily take her home."

"Now where does she live?" asked Bette.

"Down the street, near those jerks, the Williards and the Faracellis."

"But if she lives so far down, how did she see the stray money?" said Darcy.

"Like I said, the neighborhood never sleeps—eyes and ears everywhere. There's rumor that Lizzie was sort of scientist at one point, some even say she was a genius. But somehow she lost it and her ducks are all over the place. But she and that other lady, Geraldine, well they're always doing the Peeping Tom thing," said Hank as he pointed across the street. "All that woman does is sit in that perch of hers and gawk all day," Hank added.

"You mean up in that decaying widow's peak?" asked Bette.

"Yep."

"Doesn't she have anything else to do?" asked Darcy.

Hank paused and stroked his chin in thought. "You know, I remember when Gerry was a classy lady, getting all dressed up and working as some big shot at the bank."

"And then what happened?" said Bette as she cocked her head to better hear.

"Yeah, I remember when she had something going on all the time. She was very popular with the men," added Darcy.

"Your memory is right; she was a looker and very successful, but everything fell apart for her. Her brother, whom she was extremely fond of, left suddenly. Her lifelong pet golden retriever passed away, and then, if that wasn't enough, her fiancé was killed in a brutal car accident. There were rumors that the brakes had been tampered with and …" Hank's voice trailed off. He stared out the window as if waiting for the feature movie to begin.

"Was it foul play? Do you think he was murdered, Uncle Hank?" interrupted Darcy.

"What makes you think that?" said Hank as he averted his eyes, looking out the window. "But ever since, she has become a prisoner in her house. I have not seen her leave at all for some twenty years or so."

"Hey, what are these Uncle Hank?" asked Bette as she scooped up the sturdy binoculars.

"You wouldn't be doing a bit of your own snooping, would you?"

Hank rudely snatched the glasses away. "I'm just watching her watch me. A man has to fend for himself," he rationalized.

Darcy then grabbed the glasses and looked out the window.

"You're right, Uncle Hank. She's watching us right now."

But Hank did not answer. He sat near a lamp, where he twisted his glasses in various positions.

"What are you doing?" asked Bette.

"This is incredible, absolutely incredible," said Hank, scratching his chin thoughtfully.

"This woman … this card, she looks very much like your friend Bette." Hank looked up from the driver's license and credit card and stared at Bette.

"You're right. Bette and I noticed that in the car," added Darcy.

"And you know who these cards belong to?"

"No," both women responded together.

"That damn Williard family. This here is the daughter," explained Hank.

"You mean that family we've always had problems with?" asked Darcy.

"The one and only."

"So we had better get rid of it. Let me get the scissors."

"No way. These here cards are my lucky charms. We're going to have some fun with them," said Hank.

"But we've never used any of the cards before," reasoned Bette.

"But you've both done pretty much everything else, haven't you?" chided Hank.

The women were silent.

"You make coffee. I have to tend to something." Hank grabbed his pipe and pouch of Borkum-Riff smoking tobacco and went out the door.

Chapter Six

"Please, Mom, please come out," rallied Brad, Susie, and Karen. "We're sorry if we did something wrong," continued their unified plea.

"Yeah, and I need help with my history assignment," said Brad who would often procrastinate by watching his favorite cartoons.

Joliana sat on the cozy bed cushions and gazed out the window. The aging bungalow stared back at her—the place in which she had grown up and couldn't seem to get away from. Joliana pulled her short bob behind her ears and stroked the golden tendrils. She spent more time there than here. And there was so much to do in her own house. She always felt compelled to maintain her hefty schedule of cleaning and painting and rearranging the furniture just so. Then there was the bookkeeping work for the three family-shared dairy marts. She just went on and on all day, like that ridiculous Energizer bunny on television.

"Mom, please open up!" said Susie in earnest as all three pounded the door.

The phone began its vibrant jingle, and Brad and Karen scrambled down the hall to answer it. The racket was unsettling, but Joliana did not move. She had had enough today, enough of Grandpa's demands to cook, clean, and run errand upon errand; and she, being such a perfectionist, had taken too long to do everything. Gosh. She didn't finish the list. The grocery shopping would have to wait until tomorrow. And the marts, she was supposed to pick up the monies and deposit them at the bank. Oh well.

"Joliana, I need to talk to you. I got a phone call and had to rush over to see Marty," said Tony with a sense of urgency in his rich low voice.

"Now."

Something was not right. She noted a heightened irritation in her husband's tone. He was usually so patient, so accommodating.

Joliana went to the newly whitewashed door and pushed open the door lock. "What is it?" she asked pensively.

"There's been a robbery."

"A robbery, where?" asked Joliana.

"At Marty's store."

"The Marty's Complete, in Rocky Mountain?" said Joliana.

"That's the only one I know of."

"What about the other two stores?"

"The Dairy Plus and Dan's Dairy are all right, as far as I know."

"Did anyone get hurt?" asked Joliana uneasily.

"I don't think so, but Joe said the two workers were pretty shaken up."

"And about when did this happen?"

"Late last night, but Marty didn't call me until this morning," Tony said in an irritated voice.

"Last night," Joliana parroted. Why, she had been there yesterday, readying things for a bank drop.

"Something the matter?" asked Tony, noting the flushed color in his wife's cheeks.

"Uh no … oh, yes, I'm most concerned. What happened?"

"Well as far as I know, those damn crooks took whatever they could in cash and credit cards, and even a load full of chocolate. They bound and gagged Mary and Steve and put them in the back office. Then they shut down all the lights in the store."

"And where was Marty?"

"He found his two very scared employees this morning. With the snowstorm, Marty went in a bit late to open the store. But when he got there, he discovered that his best workers were tied solidly, although they had tried to free themselves for most of the night. They were pretty upset, but they're okay—just bruised egos with a little rope burn. But Marty was beside himself."

"So you're saying that this robbery really shook up Marty—cool, even-keeled Marty."

"Yeah, he found out that the heist went rapid fire and it was unnerving how these two average women could be so abrasive."

"They were women? You are sure of that?"

"Yep. They were both dressed in usual winter clothing but had worn flashy masks like those used for some sort of masquerade ball. And one of them waved around a small hand gun, but it was not fired. They didn't talk too much but the blond stuffed a lot of junk food in her pockets. All their pilfering ways made them hungry."

"What is happening now?" said Joliana in an edgy voice.

"Well, I just got back from the mart. The police are all over the place trying to find clues."

"What about those new cameras Marty just put in? Couldn't they just rewind to find the suspects?"

"The cops were working on checking out the cameras. One was smashed pretty good, the far corner one was missing a tape, and the third monitor was battered but still working. They were hoping to get some footage up and running."

"I hope they can get something working. Marty put in the best quality machinery. If it performed well, I was going to suggest we put the same cameras in the other two marts. But I guess right now we have to first deal with this robbery. Is there anything else that happened?"

"Oh, well, there's a little something, kind of funny, really. Mary threw a few jelly beans in the bag of money!"

"Jelly beans?"

"Yeah, they're the real expensive. The special-order kind."

"Well, so what?" said Joliana. She really needed to finish this conversation and check something.

"The jelly beans are a kind of bread crumb. Maybe they'll provide a lead to those jerks."

"If they don't eat all the evidence."

The phone again began its shrill ring for attention.

Tony bent over and grabbed the receiver. Finally.

Joliana quietly slipped down the carpeted staircase and grabbed her purse near the coat rack. She flung it open. Everything appeared to be in good order. Neat. Organized.

Then she drew out her everyday wallet. Her heartbeat accelerated and pounded like heavy droplets of an acute rainstorm. Everything was there. Now she fumbled nervously for her oversized wallet, the one she used for banking business.

She jerked the purse and upended it. Lipstick, eyeliner, pens, pocket tissues, and a shower of items littered the carpet.

She stared in disbelief.

Where were they? Where was her special wallet? Where were her charge card and driver's license?

Joliana slipped to her knees and sifted through the array of pocket treasures. They were gone.

Joliana winced. An electrical jolt pierced her innards, leaving her stomach queasy and her head whirling with the overload of synaptic charges.

She did not have them. She had been rushed to finish up at Marty's last night. She had compiled the money and checks, which she had planned to deposit today. Indeed, she remembered placing them in her designated business wallet that contained essentials: her credit card, license, and proper identification. Could she have accidentally left the wallet on the desk in the rear office?

Was it really possible? Could she have messed up this badly?

The sour feeling in her stomach confirmed she had.

Chapter Seven

The tiny gray-colored bungalow seemed to wear a frown with eyebrows turned down. This was evidenced by the crookedness of the black shutters and the dilapidated front railings, which hung at odd angles likened to crooked teeth. Totally uncared for, the paint was hanging in shreds, and in some areas the underling wood boards boasted a greenish, weathered look, like those structures that had been seasoned at sea. While a heavy coat of winter's fury now covered the property—not like an even canvas but with many mounds and lumps—it was not always like this. In the summer months, it was a very different picture. The front gardens flanking the house became jungle-like in growth as vine and evergreen linked branches. They had flourished in every given spot, and the thickly woven foliage wrapped itself not only on the once-decorative wrought iron picket fences but had overtaken the front steps and porch and had mounted up to the second-story windows, to the roof, and to the highest point of the chimney. The lawn became a botanist's nightmare in that every species of known weed came to reside there. Some of the inordinate growth took on the appearance of dwarfed trees. There were also some real trees, fruit-bearing ones that yielded the most foul-smelling and ugly of homegrown produce. These morello cherries were of odd sizes and variant colors of pink, white, and red. When bitten into, they left an acrid taste upon the tongue. The pears harbored warts and were terribly hard, and the apples were a peculiar crab variety that smelled inviting but were utterly tasteless. This medley of plants dumped their inedible lot to the ground, resulting in a sloppy mush that filled the nostrils with a sick, syrupy aroma.

Generally, this forsaken bungalow went unnoticed by the passerby; that is, unless it was the time of year for ghosts and goblins. Then groups of area youth would gather and cast fearful glances as they whispered among themselves. They would wonder who occupied such a place and would spin their tales of intrigue and gossip. They would point fingers as they hung close to the nearby brush, and then as if a command had been heralded, they would quickly flee.

Indeed, this decrepit dwelling belonged to a woman named Lizzie Owens.

Lizzie had become the rightful owner to the place when her parents passed on. Once their strong rein was gone, Lizzie did as she pleased. She was glad to be rid of their annoying demands, their caustic tongues, and their constant hand-slapping. She could never satisfy them; they had wanted her to fit into their standards. They had wanted her to be a sharp business woman; however, Lizzie had chosen the career of an aeronautics engineer. But her sojourn was short. She couldn't follow orders and do things according to given specifications, which was a shame considering that Lizzie's intelligence ranged in the genius level. With her propensity towards math and language, some say she may even be a savant. So she had been left jobless, much to her parents' disappointment.

But Lizzie was far from bored. She loved to learn, so reading became not only her passion but her second career. She would collect book upon book, either something from out of a nearby dumpster or a way overdue library rental. Newspapers fascinated her as well, especially articles about the town and glossy fashion articles. Yet those thick black editions of medical journals and law annals, and mathematical hardcovers, were her absolute passion. Lizzie would finger through them often, each reread leaving oily finger marks and frayed pages. All of this reading material was high in importance and found a niche in her heart and home. Lizzie never threw a shred of paper away. How could she when she may have missed a valuable article, some juicy piece of information? It had to be stored for the future, when she had the time to get to it. So the yellowed newsprint, paperbacks, and hardcovers were stored from floor to ceiling and weaved cornstalk-type rows about the tiny four rooms—just enough space in between for Lizzie to angle through. It was the maze of all mazes.

Stale, opened cans of stew and tuna contributed a sour odor that clung to rug, couch, and curtain. But it wasn't just musk and mildew from aged reading material that filled the house. Stray cats lopped about the place, adding their fur balls and cacophony of mewing. She had a soft heart for those lost, furry creatures, and her house was their house. She took good care of them, leaving them milk and remainders of dinner. Yet they were on their own after that, cleanliness was not her forte, so the cats had to stake out their own corner of piled newsprint.

Lizzie felt she was wrapped in a great comforter when she was home, with her cats and lighted candles about her. But most of the time she was not. Often, Lizzie would get the notion to go out somewhere to get something, and she would just leave. It didn't matter if she had washed or dressed appropriately as long as she had on her deep ruby lipstick. Lizzie wouldn't dare leave without it. But most important, Lizzie had to adjust her huge bug-eyed sunglasses. They were fashioned in old world styling and were exceedingly dark. They were a permanent fixture on her brow; her eyes were always shielded, and rumors and fears that she was a dangerous nutcase seemed to escalate. Some folks even claimed that she had a huge glass eye that acted as a giant magnifying glass, aiding her in her Peeping Tom behavior.

The graying, unkempt hair that hung in ringlets about her face, along with the sunglasses, lipstick, and bedraggled bedclothes, gave Lizzie a turn-of-the-century institutional look. She was the town's acting street person as she walked around heaving heavy bags of innumerable valuable items, such as books and precious discarded goods. Lizzie was not invisible like most nomadic types. Since she did not establish a regular scavenger route, she would often just show up, taking someone totally off guard. Of course, this was not Lizzie's intent, for her sole desire was to seek out her treasures and avoid any altercations. Lizzie had her own mind about things, and that was that. And right now, she wanted to pay some visits to a few of the neighborhood residents; Geraldine was first on her list.

With each ring, Geraldine could sense her blood pressure rising. And rising. It felt as if the blood volume had so increased that her skin could barely hold it all in. When would that crazy Lizzie answer? It had been an hour ago that she visited the Stallers, and she had watched her come home at least fifteen minutes ago. So why wasn't she answering?

Because crazy Lizzie wasn't all there—in the head, that is. Geraldine knew this, but knowing this did not help her impatience. If only she could march right over there. But she couldn't. Her house had been her refuge and her prison for the better part of twenty years. What was the matter with her? Every time she tried to step from the house, her heart rate would rush, she would sweat like it was the dog days of summer, and she felt like her chest was being crushed. She hated herself for it. She had even paid a banker's wage to a supposedly well-qualified psychiatrist. He had visited her frequently and sunk her bank account, with little result. Oh well.

The shrill ringing of her ancient bell system was definitely annoying. The caller was pressing the buzzer so insistently that it sounded like an urgent Morse code message. Indeed, someone else was as impatient as herself. But they would have to wait for her to ascend the winding staircase to the first level.

Geraldine gingerly peered through the eyepiece in the door. Finally. Geraldine pushed the door open. There stood a woman clad solely in a blue flannel nightgown and a gray cardigan that was three sizes too tight. Covering her feet were a pair of flowered slippers, which boasted a few too many holes. From the hem to the slipper heel, her legs were entirely bare. She pushed by Geraldine, spewing clumps of wet snow and mud on the shag carpeting. Her hair hung in oily ringlets, and her blush was haphazardly applied, as if it was done by a drunkard. Her lipstick was a smeared ruby red, making her look much like a young child who had devoured candy apples.

Lizzie Owens had arrived.

"It's about time," Geraldine muttered irately.

"I'll take that as a greeting," said Lizzie as she adjusted her large, dark-rimmed glasses. They were her signature item. She never took them off; her eyes were forever shrouded in mystery.

"Well, I saw you at the Stallers a few minutes ago and …"

"Yes, I did as you had requested," said Lizzie. "I went over to find out what was going on."

"And what did you discover?" asked Geraldine, her right eyebrow twitching nervously.

Lizzie ignored the comment. A chiseled look of determination arched her cheek bone as she thoroughly searched the living room—under chairs, behind the sofa, in the closet.

"Lizzie, what on earth are you doing?"

"Can't you see that I'm conducting an official investigation? I need to ascertain whether there is additional evidence here. There's a quadrillion fingerprints all over the place, and that's an amount that starts with a one followed by fifteen zeros. I will have to go home to get the special dusting powder." Lizzie paused as she looked to the side of the china cabinet. "Maybe I won't have to, because our fugitive is hiding behind here. Actually, you may have to leave the room because I believe that this culprit is from Venus, which means he spits poisonous bile, which, of course, I have the keen olfactory nerves to sense."

"You are doing what and I have to go where?" said Geraldine as she rubbed her fingertips together. She knew Lizzie to be quite the eccentric; she being a genius could do that to a person.

Lizzie began sniffing like a dog. "I can also smell those stress hormones. Don't you know that adrenaline make sweat glands pump out a prodigious amount of the musky stuff, generally in the under arms?"

Geraldine gave a bewildered look to her friend as she watched the search step up in intensity. Cushions, newspapers and decorative items went flying.

"Now, Lizzie, that's quite enough," shouted Geraldine as she positioned herself eye to eye with the eccentric woman.

"Move, you amorphous mass; you're impeding my serious work as a private investigator on a crime scene."

"You are what? A private investigator, a PI? That's what you think you are?" Geraldine's words came fast, bold and fully annunciated. "You are not any such thing. Remember the last time you were a radio announcer and you got us in trouble with the newspaper people! Now snap out of it!" Geraldine barked.

"Please be quiet. I need quiet to operate assiduously so I could disentangle the nefarious plot so that I will ..."

Geraldine abruptly pulled the soft fabric from Lizzie's shoulder and shouted in her ear. She had had enough of Lizzie's stubborn ways and complicated vocabulary. "Stop it, now!" shrieked Geraldine. She crossed her arms and stood her ground like an army sergeant. Her marbled lavender eyes flashed lightning bolts at Lizzie.

Lizzie bristled. That voice—it was so scary, so commanding. She knew that voice. Lizzie's shoulders then slumped, and her arms fell listlessly to her side.

"I'm so very sorry," said Lizzie in a gentle voice as she wrapped her arms around Geraldine's waist. "I didn't mean it. I won't ever be so silly again."

Geraldine gasped as she pulled away from the boa constrictor embrace. She took in a deep breath.

"That's okay, Lizzie. Now why don't we sit and have some tea?"

"I'd like that very much, Miss Geraldine," said Lizzie as she made her way to the dining table. Then she began pulling on her pajamas. "Where did I put it?" she muttered over and over.

Geraldine studied the odd woman. She noticed a bulge in the sweater pocket.

"Lizzie, how about you check your sweater, it seems to me ..."

Lizzie wasted no time yanking at her tattered pockets, tearing the right side so that it hung by a thread. Several twenty dollar bills and two fifties fell onto the plush carpet.

"Well, what's this?" asked Geraldine.

"I found the bills in the snow outside the Staller house. I was thinking of giving them back. I did walk close to the house, but then I changed my mind."

"Why?"

"Finders keepers, that's why," said Lizzie smugly.

"Well, for whatever reason, I am glad you kept the money. I think this is evidence of something wrong."

"But, Geraldine, it's only money. Maybe Mr. Staller dropped it, that's all.

"No, I think something is up at the Stallers'."

"I think that you're overreacting, acting like a cop or something."

"Perhaps you're right, Lizzie. This whole thing is just a misunderstanding." Geraldine bent over to scoop up the scattered currency. Smooth hands with long fuchsia-colored nails tore past Geraldine and snatched the bills. But Geraldine held tight to a crisp fifty.

"Let go!" demanded Lizzie.

"I won't. You let go, you crazy woman!" shrieked Geraldine.

"I found it fair and square," argued Lizzie.

"Yes. I told you to go over to the Stallers, so I was the one …"

"Who made me an errand clerk ," said Lizzie, finishing the comment. "I'm sick of doing all these things for you. 'Lizzie, get my mail, buy me a newspaper, find out what is happening over at the Stallers'!'"

Both women stubbornly pulled on the bill.

It tore in half!

Each gazed at her hand, perplexed and annoyed.

A thundering knock, like the fist of a giant, slammed on the oak door. "Open up the door, Ms. Pryor … Geraldine—whatever your name is! Open it, now!"

Lizzie quickly deposited the money in her torn sweater pocket and boldly walked to the door.

Geraldine stepped ahead of the flannel-clad woman. "Don't even think of opening that door! That's Mr. Staller, that crazy man!"

"I think we should be decent and at least find out what he wants."

"What he wants!" hissed Geraldine, "I'll tell you what he wants!"

"Ladies, yes, ladies, I can hear you both in there," yelled Mr. Staller, "Yes, Geraldine, or may I say snoopy Gerry and her cohort the nutty Ms. Lizzie? Now you had better open this door!"

Silence.

Both ladies froze, like French ladies in waiting, except for Geraldine's eyes, which were twitching, and Lizzie's hands, which were shaking.

"You crazy broads, I know all about your neighborhood snooping. Yes, Geraldine, you may not know it, but the entire street can see your bobbing nest of hair in that widow's peak you live in; and you, Lizzie, yes, I saw you come in a few minutes ago. Well, woman, you were trespassing in my yard," ranted Hank.

Geraldine and Lizzie waited. Their breath hung in suspended vapors.

"Open up, you two," bellowed Hank as he pounded on the door.

The door shook and creaked, and it seemed to be easing from its very molding.

"Okay, so don't open the door, but if either one of you comes near my place again, it won't be pretty!"

Heavy boots bounded from the porch, down the front stairs.

Geraldine and Lizzie crept lightly to the picture window and lifted the edge of the delicate curtain. They watched Hank stomp out to his peeling blue pickup, his long gray hair sticking out of his cap. Moments later, tires screeched and mud and snow flew as he raced off.

Geraldine turned to Lizzie. "Now you can go. I think you better make it quick, before he returns."

Lizzie nodded and headed towards the door.

"Let me help you," said Geraldine as she took the arm of the older woman and slyly slipped the crunched bills from Lizzie's torn pocket to her own.

No one would ever get the better of her.

Chapter Eight

"Oh, this ridiculous pan!" Joliana muttered as she attacked the stained pot with the scouring pad.

"Something the matter?" asked her husband as he grabbed a towel to come help her wipe dishes.

"No, no, I'm all right. It's just the kids burned the macaroni and cheese and now this pan is a mess."

"We'll soak it awhile, and I'll do it later," said Tony. "Besides, there's more fun things to do," he said as he playfully tossed her hair and blew into her ear.

"Yeah, yeah, I'm in no mood. I need to finish this pan. If only you hadn't let the kids start dinner."

"But you were so upset."

"And I have a right to be angry, with my dad demanding so much of me, and then to find out that we've been robbed."

"Honey, we weren't robbed. That was my nephew's store."

"Well, he's family, and it's only a matter of time until our mart gets hit."

"Now, now," interrupted Tony, his voice more edgy, "you know our mart is much more visible and that Marty's business is out in the boonies."

"Yeah, I know, but this whole situation bothers me."

"Me too. I'd like to find those thugs and give them a piece of my mind," said Tony, his attempt at being even-keeled suddenly erupting.

"Hey, now look at this!" said Joliana, proudly lifting the glistening pan for him to see. "Just like new." She really didn't want to get him out of sorts, especially now.

"Just great," said Tony sarcastically as he tossed the towel to the side and headed towards the living room.

Sometime later, Joliana peeked into the living room. A happy chaos was going on, with Tony playing bronco with their youngest, and the other two dancing and singing to the blaring stereo. Now was her chance. She scribbled out a brief note and left it smack in the middle of the kitchen table. Then she was out the door.

It seemed that every second, she was checking her watch. Generally, closing time was nine o'clock, and she figured she would get there with a little time to spare. She pressed down on the gas and watched the speedometer rise. "Oh, great," she said aloud. First she lied to her husband, and now she was speeding, speeding without a license. She was becoming a genuine outlaw.

Joliana slowly turned into the parking lot of Marty's Complete. While it was generally a neon light amidst intertwined hemlocks and oak, tonight it was different. There was a hush about the place. The sole light was the reflection of her high beams in the store's picture window. "Damn," she said aloud. She should have known better. Of course the place would be closed down with the robbery last night and the police around the place like flies.

Then she saw a flicker.

She killed her light beams and peered into the darkness.

Had she imagined it?

No, there it was again. A tiny light was moving inside the mart. Joliana eased herself carefully from the car and approached the entrance. Everything was pitch dark and her eyes were not adjusting. If there was anyone in that store, they already had a decent view of her.

Her feet then got snarled in a thick yellow tape that boldly stated, "Keep Out Crime Scene." Why was it on the ground? The front door was ajar, propped open by a muddy brick that had been eased from the landscaping. *Hmm, this is interesting, very interesting.*

She saw the flicker again.

And it saw her. The glow of iridescent lights danced and twirled right towards her.

Joliana gasped.

A police car silently slid into the clearing, its flashes throwing an eerie red and blue glow on the scene.

Joliana carefully groped her way back to her car. All she had to do was trip on a stray twig and fall face first—what would she say to the police officer? "I came for milk"? Moments later, she slammed her foot on the gas pedal and propelled out of there.

It was a good thing the Family Diner was still open. Joliana discretely pulled her two-tone brown and terribly muddied Volvo station wagon into the front of the restaurant. She sat a moment and peered out her rearview mirror.

No one was behind her.

Gosh, she thought that the police car would have tailed her, but there was absolutely no sign of it. She should be grateful, but all she could feel was a kind of foreboding, like someone was about to drop a black cloth over her head and smother her.

Joliana stepped from the car. A tingling sensation reached at each root of her hair and then down her spine. She could sense someone was watching her.

She stood immobilized in the frosty air and listened. Nothing. Nothing but the wind that was finding its way between each thread of her woolen jacket. She headed for the diner.

"Hot tea. Yes, hot tea and blueberry pie would be fine," she told the waitress moments later. She settled into her cozy booth and looked around. Not too many people—an elderly couple over there, an older gentleman on her right, a couple of teenagers on the other side. No one she knew, thank goodness.

Her order came, and, with gusto, Joliana consumed the comfort food. The tea was so warm it eased her hunched shoulders, and her mind seemed less cobwebby.

Now why had she been so clumsy last night? She had left her business wallet with her major credit card and license with the monies to be dropped at the bank. She had meant to slip it all in her purse so she could visit the bank the next day. How could she have been so sloppy? Joliana stirred more lemon and honey into her tea and reenacted the moment in her mind. She was always so attentive to detail that her husband would say that they were Oscar and Felix, the neat fanatic opposite the slob. There was some kind of distraction. Yes, yes, that was it. In her peripheral vision, she had seen two women, and one looked very familiar to her. She didn't know quite why. So she had stepped from the rear office to watch them. One woman was disheveled, her dirty blond hair pulled back, her jeans and jacket ill-fitting and dirty. The other woman was a bit more put-together, but her fashion statement was black and forbidding.

But it was the first woman's mouth that bothered her.

Since Joliana had always been a stickler about dental health, for herself and her family, she would never forget that mouth. As the woman conversed with her friend, the decay of tooth and gum was apparent. There was enough repair work in that mouth alone for a dentist to retire, Joliana had mused.

Nervously, Joliana fingered the sugar substitutes. Those two women had seemed suspicious to her. Could it be possible that they were the same women who robbed the store but had visited first to survey the situation or, as they say in the movies, case the joint?

"Miss, would you like anything else—a muffin or a refill of tea?" asked the seasoned waitress.

"Ah, I would love more tea, please," said Joliana.

As Joliana steeped the fresh tea bag, she let the warm vapors flood her cheek. *Hmmm...*

So the story was simple. She had had a very frustrating day, but it was those two women who had greatly distracted her. So she had left without taking the monies and her cards. Then why did she still feel uneasy? Joliana realized that while she held a single ray of understanding, her peripheral view remained dark and foreboding.

Joliana took in a deep breath and let it out slowly. She let out all the tension. Yet her fingers had a mind of their own, as all the sugar packets, white, blue, and yellow, were organized and arranged just so.

The phone was ringing on and on.

"Hey, hon, can you get that?" shouted Tony as he playfully wrestled with the children. It was his turn on the bottom of the pile, while Susie and Brad teasingly pummeled his chest. Tony's full cheeks were flushed, and his clear blue eyes boasted of adventure. The more cautious Karen, not wanting to wreck her manicure, stood to the side and cheered them on.

"Go Susie, go Brad. You've got Dad. He can't escape you now."

Between the rowdy horseplay and peals of laughter, the jingle of the phone annoyingly continued.

"C'mon, hon, will you get that?"

Still no answer.

"I'll get it, Dad," said Karen as she danced over to the phone.

"Is that you, Joliana? Where are you?" Joe's tone was curt and caustic.

"Grandpa, you can say hello to me," said Karen curtly. "So you're looking for Mom ..."

"You got that right. I've been waiting here for my dinner, and she was supposed to bring it over an hour ago."

"Well, I didn't know Mom was bringing you dinner. Let me go find her. You know, Grandpa, with all the calls you make to Mom, she should have one of those special cell phones. "

Tony grabbed the phone. He hated the way his father-in-law treated his kids and his wife—so damn demanding.

"Yeah, Joe, what's up?"

"Nothing. I want to talk to Joliana."

"Well you can ask me," said Tony in an irritated tone.

"I want the dinner I was promised."

"I didn't know Joliana promised you supper tonight. I thought she made you lunch today and you are invited to dinner on Sunday."

"Hey, can't an old man just get something to eat? Let me talk to Joliana," said Joe in an ornery manner.

"I won't have you pushing my wife around like that. She'll be over when she's good and ready you cantankerous old fart!"

A loud click ended the conversation. *Darn*, thought Tony. He was just getting the nerve to give that codger a piece of his mind.

"Honey, where are you?"

No answer.

Tony went around the first floor, stopping near the kitchen. He leaned over the banister of the winding staircase. "Joliana, are you upstairs?" Tony shouted. His eye then landed on a note perched on the middle of the table. It was addressed to him.

Tony unfolded the paper, his attention caught by one word: apologize. He quickly reread the abbreviated note. Joliana had gone out to her cousin Alice's house, or so she said. Why would she apologize for that? Since when did he ever interfere with her relationship with Alice? He was totally baffled but he wouldn't be for long as he reached for the house address book.

Joe stomped around his kitchen, muttering to himself. He opened a cabinet and threw cans of soup, beef stew, and noodles on the counter. *Great*, he thought, *blood pressure in a can*. There was so much sodium, his bloodstream would be more laden then the Dead Sea.

"Now where the hell is that can opener?" Joe said aloud, sifting through this drawer and that. "I can't believe she did this to me, after all I've done for her."

His thick hands encircled the can as he attempted to pry the lid off. It wasn't coming off clean at all. *Why can't they make a can opener that really works?* The antiquated rusted opener slid, causing Joe's thumb to land on the jagged edge.

"Damn! I've done it now!" bellowed Joe, as he grabbed a dish towel to stop the bleeding.

A few minutes later, he surveyed the rudimentary bandage job he had done. The wrapping on his thumb was somewhat similar to the thick bindings of an Egyptian mummy.

The phone began its shrill beckoning.

"I'm coming, I'm coming," said Joe. "Maybe it's Joliana, with an apology and a wonderful home-cooked meal."

Hastily picking up the receiver, he said crisply, "So now you've come to your senses. My appetite's been waiting."

Someone was breathing but not saying a word.

"I know you're there!" said Joe.

Then he heard a click. Whoever it was had gone. Oh well, another prank call. He seemed to get them all the time.

Joe eased himself back into the well-worn leather chair. He leaned back and, with his right hand, stroked the hairs of his salt-and-pepper beard. He had done this forever, to think, but he had been completely unaware of this habit until his wife mentioned it. She would often laugh and chide him about his constant chin stroking.

Joe stared ahead at the desk full of clutter. He hadn't bothered to tidy anything since his wife had died, for he had only done so because of her constant nagging. However, Joliana had often offered an ultimatum that if he didn't get working on it, then she would do so. But absolutely not! This was his space, his special nook in the house. But maybe itwas time to do a bit of spring cleaning himself, even if it was still snowing outside. He wasn't hungry anymore, and this would give him something to do.

Where to start?

Piles were unevenly placed everywhere: on the desk, to the side of the sprawling cherry piece, and even in the leg space underneath. Mail, manila envelopes, and old dusty paperbacks were strewn between. There were two of his favorite coffee mugs perched here and there.

Joe lifted the cup and his lip curled in disgust. Something greenish-black and fuzzy was growing. Darn. And these were some great mugs. *Well,* he thought, *why not start in the middle.* He thrust his good hand into the pile and came out with two Christian magazines. "Ugh," he groaned. This kind of stuff was planted throughout his house. Good grief! Joliana must consider him some kind of lost sinner who would fall into a hellish pit someday. She was constantly complaining about his lifestyle, how messy he was, how he made poor choices. Joe chuckled to himself. Sometimes she would go all nuts on him and start yelling when he did things she thought were crazy. Like last week, when he took a couple pounds of old fish and went and threw it around the park. Good fertilizer. Or a few weeks ago, before the big snow fully hardened the ground, he had taken his shovel and buried his ever faithful ol' yeller in the backyard. He laughed aloud. The antiquated radio that he had played at full volume had finally given out. A decent burial had been the right thing to do. The there was the washing of his underwear and black socks in the tub with barefoot agitation, like the early Italian wine crushers.

Joliana absolutely flipped out. She liked everything perfect, all lined up just so, with not a speck of dust anywhere. It wasn't human the way his daughter lived. Joe sighed. Perhaps he had given the wrong one away; maybe the other girl was more like him. But no need to cry over burned toast. What was done was done. There was no way to recall it as one would with a lemon of a car. It had been a tough decision, full of regret and recrimination. But that all happened a long time ago, although at times, it seemed like the closeted adoption happened yesterday. Joe tossed books and folders aside and then decided to try the three drawers. The first came out easily, clinking about with pens and pencils and an odd assortment of stationary supplies. The second was not as easy. With his workable hand, he gave a few hearty twists. The cherry drawer dislodged, but halfway through its journey, manila envelopes snagged the top runners. Joe pulled again and was finally able to release it. Joe groaned. Now he remembered that this was the important drawer that held every piece of valuable paperwork, from his childhood report cards to his marriage documents, adoption papers, and personal will and testament. His wife had often scolded him for not securing it all downtown in a security box. But how safe are banks anyway? These documents had done just fine. Joe grabbed a handful of the papers and slammed them on the desk. He would read and weed later. But right now, he was interested in checking out the third drawer; he had a hunch he knew what was in it. Joe pulled at the lower-level drawer. It refused to move. He tugged a little harder. The drawer shuddered a bit but remained as if Super-Glued in place. The third time, Joe threw his left foot against the drawer to loosen it, and then, with his right hand, yanked with all his might.

The drawer sprang open.

Joe could hardly believe his senses. His hunch had been right. There before him, wedged between bills and letters, was a genuine Smith &Wesson. The real McCoy.

Chapter Nine

"Honest to Pete, I can't stand that jerk down the street," said Hank as he stomped the snow and mud from his boots.

Bette and Darcy looked up from the table, which was hastily strewn with sandwich fixings; condiment lids were spread about and chip bags rashly ripped open.

"Wow, looks like you girls wasted no time stuffing your faces," continued Hank.

"Well, we waited for you, but when you didn't come back, we couldn't help ourselves," said Bette as she wiped the mayonnaise from her lip.

"Yeah, and Hank, we did wait, but what took you so long? We've been sitting and watching your antique of a television for hours. How in the world do you watch all that white blur?" asked Darcy.

"Yeah, I even took a bath and dozed for a couple of hours," said Bette.

"Long? I was only gone ten minutes. And I come back to find I've been eaten out of my own house."

"What's that you got there?" asked Bette.

Hank took the mildew-encrusted cardboard box and slung it onto the table.

"Have a look and see," he said.

Bette moved her chair back a bit. "Gosh that thing stinks. I'm trying to eat here!"

"Bette, now don't get all sissy on me," said Darcy as she pulled on the rusty zipper. She peered inside. "Looks like someone's full four years of school junk."

"There's more than that. Take a look at the book to the side. Yes, that one," directed Hank.

Darcy held up a thick blue book with fancy edging and calligraphy that spelled out a date and high school. With her hand, she wiped away the dust and grime. "Yep, just what I thought; it's a yearbook. So what of it?"

"Open it."

"Okay, I'm looking through it, but it's just a bunch of dumb high school graduates."

"I wouldn't say that. You might have been one of those dumb graduates."

Darcy flipped to the cover and reread the dates. "So, what of it? I didn't make it."

"Yeah, but someone else did. Look just under the Ws," directed Hank.

Darcy quickly fingered the sodden pages to names beginning with W. "Watson, Wazer, Weston, Williard. Holy cow, what do we have here!" Darcy stared down at the page. Bette left her feast and plopped her greasy potato chip finger on the picture.

"Hey!" exclaimed Bette. "That woman looks like me. I mean, she's way younger and has lighter hair, but we are very much alike."

"Wrong," said Darcy, "she's not way younger. This is her yearbook, so that would make her hmm ... thirty-three or so."

"And I'm thirty-two. And a half."

"Exactly," said Darcy.

"Yeah, but Darcy, this woman has such a pretty smile and mine . . . well, you know mine."

Darcy stared down at the page. Bette left her oversized sandwich and sloppily wiped the excess mayo on her cheek onto her shirtsleeve.

Darcy and Hank both eyed Bette's mouth.

"Smile for me!" demanded Hank.

Bette clamped her teeth shut and nodded.

"Now!" shouted Hank.

Bette gave a smirk and then threw her hand to her mouth.

"Disgusting," said Hank. "Your mouth is worse than mine. It looks like you've got gooey pea soup stuck to your teeth."

"So they both look alike except for some simple cosmetics, but the mouth is a dead giveaway," said Darcy. Then she cast a discerning eye between the yearbook and her friend. "Her hair is more blond than yours. You have a lot more mousy brown."

"Yeah, so I guess I can't be parading around as her after all," added Bette.

"Well, if you put a lid on your mouth and got a dye job, you could," said Hank.

"You're not kidding about this, Uncle Hank," said Darcy.

A mischievous smile arched Hank's unkempt moustache, and his eyes twitched with boyish menace. He rubbed the tops of his fingers together.

"I'm certainly not. This will be very fine indeed," Hank added.

"And it's not about the money, is it, Hank?" said an irritated Bette.

"No, it's not," interjected Darcy. "He's had it in for this family for many years."

"But what happened to make you so angry?"

Hank shrugged and did not answer. Lost in thought, he studied the young woman in the picture. Then he tossed the license photo at Bette, along with a cheap ballpoint pen. "Stop yakking and get working at copying this signature. This woman writes like a school teacher, so you'll have to try hard."

"So, Hank, you really are serious about pulling off a crazy heist using Bette to pose as Joliana?"

Darcy stood so close to her uncle that she could caught strong waves of tobacco breath mixed with coffee. "Well?"

"Tomorrow morning we'll do something. But first, Bette needs to get the handwriting right." Hank began to rummage through a pile of mail on the counter and found several sheets of clean typewriter paper. "Show me what you can do, and we'll talk later." Hank turned and went into the living room. Within moments, he sunk into his favorite Duct-taped leather chair and gazed at a blaring, static-filled, black-and-white television. He relit his favorite pipe, and grunted and groaned at each slam dunk.

Bette opened her mouth in rebuttal but noted Darcy's pursed lips. Darcy was not a woman to be argued with just now, and she didn't want to try Hank either. Reluctantly, Bette positioned the pen between her thumb and forefinger and set to work. Somewhere she had read that most people don't write exactly the same every time, but Joliana appeared to be the exception to that rule. She took a piece of clean paper and attempted to trace the name to get a feel for it. Then she tried to duplicate it on her own. Still sloppy. Not quite right. She repeated the process, her head tucked down as the long tendrils of her hair hid her determined grimace. With each stroke, the charm bracelet clanged on the table.

"Hey, take off that damn jewelry. You're doing an awful job," said Darcy as she leaned over Bette's shoulder.

Bette shrugged and repositioned herself, using her left arm to shield the paper. The jangle of the stolen golden bracelet was harsh and irritating.

"Go ahead and ignore me, but you'll find out what a pathetic mess you're making!" Darcy snatched up a nearby newspaper and headed into the bedroom to read.

Both women were so engrossed that neither heard when Hank slipped out into the frigid winter night.

Chapter Ten

WEDNESDAY

Joliana angled one cart with her right arm and pulled the other from the rear. Other patrons avoided the Mack-truck-like configuration in the aisle. Indeed, her dogged determination and mountainous load of groceries made her a colossal force to reckon with. That was her well put-together outside. Inside, a well-rigged explosion was hurling concrete slobs at her. She shouldn't even be in this damned grocery store, but the five phone calls from her dad had pushed her buttons. She had been in the middle of things, attempting to dismantle her house and then efficiently replace everything. "Now where are they?" she muttered aloud. She had pulled every book out of the bookcase, explored all the obscure corners and side-swiped cushions. Nothing. Absolutely nothing. No cards. Both the license and charge card were still missing. Now she was pretty sure they weren't in the house. She had checked the store premises last night but couldn't get in. By now, one of the store workers would have called her if they had noticed the cards fallen off the desk. That is, if that other party hadn't found them first.

"Miss, did you want a half or full pound of that cheese?" asked the deli clerk.

"Ah, a pound should do," Joliana mumbled.

"White or yellow?"

"White."

"Thick or thin?"

Joliana looked down at both carts. Everything was organized and evenly distributed, with items all categorized: the dairy here, the produce over there, the canned goods in the far corner. But to her dismay, she realized she had forgotten many items, and she was scheduled to book-keep for the other two stores in just an hour.

"Thick or thin?" the clerk repeated the question, her candied demeanor taking on a sour edge as she waved a slice in her hand.

"That's fine, thank you," replied Joliana. She really was in no mood for all this.

Now she had to backtrack. No ketchup. Dad needed it for his eggs. She should have been watching her list. *Why even write such an elaborate list if you're not going to use it?* Joliana tugged the carriages and pushed to gain momentum.

The cards, the cards—where are they? She had to find them quickly before someone went out and had a party. She hoped her husband wasn't home. He would just belittle for her stupidity. Gosh, she was always trying to do things just right. Why had it gone so wrong? She knew Tony had waited up for her last night, but he had fallen asleep in his favorite high-backed chair. In the morning, she had found his concerned note. He wanted to talk when he got home. What would she say? She felt so irresponsible. She always kept things in good order. She couldn't bear him thinking less of her, or even worse, yelling at her. She didn't want to talk to him. Oh well.

Joliana pulled several kinds of cereal off the shelves. Highway robbery. She smirked. However, they sold such items at their mart for substantially more, and selections were limited. So she really shouldn't talk. Darn. Her thoughts were all over the place. She had to think about where the cards were. She had to figure how to explain this blunder with her husband. She needed more time to think and to look. First thing's first: she would get these groceries squared away with her dad. Then she would make some excuse and call the Woodbridge Mart to say she could not book-keep today. Gosh, juggling these three marts was such a chore anyhow, and with the robbery at Marty's Mart, her mundane bookkeeping seemed so trivial. What could they say? After all, it was their family business; she could do what she wanted. Joliana's tightened neck muscles eased just a bit. At least she had a plan.

The air was redolent with the spicy scent of musks and floral sprays. Bette was delighted with the sampling choices. She sprayed a bit behind her woolen red cap and some on her wrist.

"Bette, c'mon, you're making a spectacle of yourself!"

"Darcy, this stuff smells so good."

"Bette, we're on a mission. We have to get going!"

"Wow, Dar, our cart is full of stuff. Who cares about a little perfume?"

"We've got these expensive contraptions Hank wanted, but we have to find more clothing!"

"There's plenty of clothing in there."

"I mean, Bette, more Joliana clothing."

"But besides the dark pants and deep blue pea jacket, and, of course, this woolen hat, what else do we know about her? We only saw her for a quick second yesterday, shoveling snow."

"Well then, let's just get one more pair of pants, and then we'll go to the next store."

"Next store?"

"Yeah, Uncle Hank wanted a new snow blower and some specialty tools."

"Expensive stuff."

"That's the idea."

"Can this be traced?"

Darcy ignored her friend's comment. "Then we'll go grab some Spiegel catalogs and spend some time on the phone."

Bette smiled widely. "We're gonna ring up a pretty penny."

"Not if you do that," admonished Darcy. "Keep your mouth shut when we go through the counter."

"Ah ..." a gray shadow flickered through Bette's lovely jade eyes. It was her bad teeth again—always her bad teeth.

"And pull that cap a bit more over your head."

"I hate when you order me around, Darcy."

"I know, Bette, but we need some Clairol and improved glamour on you before the big time."

"And this isn't?"

Darcy shrugged. She had felt it premature to be out here so soon, but Hank had pressed and pressed. He said they had a fleeting window of opportunity on the cards. So they outfitted Bette with a woolen cap and found an old coat. The remainder of the evening, Bette had sat, pen in hand, attempting to capture the fine nuances of Joliana's signature. She had labored over her penmanship, her tongue sliding from one corner of her mouth to the other. Then the bracelet slammed on the counter.

Darcy held her breath.

Bette raised her pen from the paper. Hardly glancing at the card, the cashier nodded, smiled, and handed it back to Bette.

First mission accomplished.

Darcy grabbed a bag and pushed in the expensive cologne bottle. She chuckled. So Bette had grabbed a perfume or two. So what? They had gotten what they came for. These were just small potatoes. She couldn't wait to get to the next store.

Identity theft. Hank understood it to be quite lucrative. It was getting easier nowadays, especially with pushy telemarketers. Hell, with all the pre-approved credit card applications being sent to disinterested people, all he would have to do is scout out a few garbage cans and he could have a party. Also, he had heard that with Social Security cards and a home computer, a savvy operator could access bank records, passwords, place of birth, addresses, phone numbers, and a mother's maiden name—the whole shooting match. That is, if he wanted to. Hank smiled as he climbed down the rickety stairs to the basement. He angled his flashlight at his feet to create a relatively safe passageway through all the piles of accumulated living, which held a thick inch of dust. Damn, even the compacted earthen floor held a layer of soot. He came upon a far corner of the room where a dingy pull-chain fell from a precariously placed light bulb. He gave the chain a tug. One, two flickers. The timeworn wattage struggled to come alive. Another flash and it went on as it swayed dangerously from the loose, frayed fixture.

Now to check this out. The swaying bulb created moving shadows, which made creepy monsters out of the most ordinary things, like the chipped armoire with some old two-by-fours thrown over the top; it looked like a creepy creature with horns. Hank was not spooked in the least. Such creatures were in storybooks for the feeble of heart. What bothered him more were those around him. That called themselves refined, called themselves progressive, called themselves neighbors. Now they were the real enemy. Hank grabbed the dank-smelling army blanket and threw it to the side. A wicker clothes hamper sat innocently before him. It had once been a daffodil color, but with the years of intense cold and heat, a combination of chalky and sooty mold covered its surface.

Identity theft. Indeed, he had sent his niece and her friend on such a mission. And why not? They could make a fast killing with that card and nothing would give him better satisfaction. Hank didn't care for this kind of robbery; it wasn't his style. But it had everything to do with his contempt towards that Williard family, especially Joe. Taking his daughter Joliana on the credit card ride of her life gave Hank a smug sense of revenge. Oh no, this rivalry had little to do with cows and property lines, like everyone thought. It went much deeper. Hank positioned the flashlight near the smelly hamper and held his breath.

It was still there. He had to be careful, so he had moved it to this spot a few months ago. Hank glanced at his wrist. Darcy and Bette would be back soon. He always felt comforted when he held the canvas bag in his hands, its contents measuring his life's accomplishment. He had better get to work.

Chapter Eleven

Joliana held her foot as far down as she could on the gas petal. She had to get home now. The groceries tumbled and swayed in the hatch; cans were rolling about, knocking into each other and who knows what else—hopefully not the eggs, especially her father's eggs. She loved her dad, but these days, he was just so demanding. "Jo this. Jo that." Taking care of the bills, the laundry, the groceries, and the commands was like an endless relay race. Once she approached the finish line, it started all over again. And that didn't include her family. Sometimes the kids get the short end of the stick—a mother who wore so many hats that her energy seemed to get all used up. Then there were the marts. Darn! Joliana hit the steering wheel with the gloved palm of her hand and piloted towards home. She had forgotten to stop and make a call. She wanted to rearrange those hours without Tony's input. Time was needed at home. Joliana pulled over to the gas station and headed towards the phone booth. It was in shambles. Metal hardware was missing and rust was showing in spots. Wires were dangling. This was definitely not a top-of-the-line cell phone. Joliana wished she hadn't balked at these convenient newfangled inventions. Oh well.

Joliana sloppily took the turn onto her street and then slowed down. A red ball had maneuvered its way towards her. She lifted her foot from the accelerator. Goodness, why play with balls in the winter? Why not sled down a hill or make a snowman or something? But usually a ball meant kids, some youngster who was not concerned about looking both ways. Just then, a young boy, his ample parka not zipped, came running out from behind a snow mound. He grabbed the ball, turned, and ran back. He never even noticed her. She had been right. Granted, it may have been a kind of mother's intuition, mostly because she had a few kids of her own.

A truck flew down the street towards her. Joliana lightly tapped the gas to grant him room, as the two vehicles rubbed the snow banks they flanked. Joliana stared at the vehicle. She knew this old, beaten-up jalopy. It was Hank's. But Hank was not driving it. Who was the driver? Joliana squinted from the sun's intense rays on the snow and came face-to-face with the passenger. The young woman had just removed her red cap, and her matted hair fell to her shoulders. The woman's eyes widened in astonishment and she lowered her head.

"Who was that woman, anyway?" Joliana wondered aloud. She looked awfully familiar for someone she had never seen before. She turned and viewed the truck angling its way into Hank's driveway. *Hmmm. Someone who knows Hank.* Yet that cantankerous man had seemed quite solitary all these years. Who could be visiting? It wasn't her business. Why should she care? Joliana eased the aging station wagon into her own driveway and again glanced down the street. Only the upper portion on the house could be seen, and it seemed quiet. *Just mind your own business,* she cajoled herself. She would let her father have it out with the Stallers. She wanted peace.

Hank needn't have worried. He began pulling out old rags and newspapers from the mildewed clothes hamper. While the papers were discolored and dank-smelling, they were quite dry. Hank went to hurl one crumpled piece when he hesitated. He had used these newspapers. What had he been thinking? There, in the black and white photo, were the police, escorting Pete away. Hank scanned the article. It was just as he remembered. Pete had been caught, but even though he was pressured by police, he had kept his wits about him. The article noted that the authorities held suspicions that Pete had accomplices and that somehow his partners in crime had hidden the stolen cash. Yet they had no proof. Pete had locked down tighter than Fort Knox. He didn't tell. He didn't crack under the pressure. But Pete became the fall guy. They couldn't find any evidence of the stolen money, but it was the murder that locked him away. That young teller had just been a bit too nervous for him. Poor Pete. He had been behind hideous concrete walls for some twenty years or so. He had been in his mid-forties then. Pete had been much younger than himself and Joe. Hank could feel his heart flutter and his face flush. That clown Joe was yellow through and through. Joe had bailed so fast during the bust. Why, if Hank hadn't had some quick thinking, he would have become Pete's jailmate. He wasn't looking at peccadilloes. This here was a serious matter. It still was, but Hank had had his vengeance.

The three-way share was altered to just a two-way, between him and Pete. Joe was cut out. Joe had argued that it was his precise ways, his cleverness that pulled it off in the first place. Maybe so. Joe had had the idea to dress as superheroes. So he had the missus design the costumes he had dreamed up for a supposed Halloween prank. They were simple and efficient and pretty darn nice. Hank chuckled. Pete had been Superman, Joe had been Spider Man, and he had been Batman. A prick of excitement tingled his spine. That bank heist had been such a hoot. So scary and so much fun. Risking it all, he had loved every minute of it.

Hank dug deeper in the large hamper. He pulled out an outdated, coffee-colored, leather briefcase.

The case was intact. It had weathered the years quite well. Hank removed the key from his pocket and inserted it. With a click to the right, he popped the case open. Hank flung the lid wide open. His smile was even grander. It was just as he had left it. He gingerly snatched up a banded bundle and flicked it like a deck of cards. It looked like it was all secure, but it would be nice to just check.

What was that? Hank twisted his head towards the far side of the cellar. Movement. Chairs upstairs scraped the kitchen's bruised floors. Excited voices and boisterous laughter followed. Oh darn. The girls were back. Darcy and Bette were certainly gloating.

"Uncle Hank, are you down there?" yelled Darcy.

Hank stood very still. What should he do?

"C'mon, Uncle Hank. We've checked the house, your van is outside, and you left the cellar door open. Please come up and see," said Bette.

"Yeah, Uncle Hank, we had a great time. We have to show you our loot. So come up or I'll come down!" teased Darcy.

"And we could use your help getting in all the heavy stuff," said Bette.

"Just a minute!" shouted Hank. "I'm looking for something, and I think I just found it!" said Hank as he quickly threw the case in the hamper and tossed in the crumpled newspapers. He tossed an army blanket over it and then an old box of five-and-dime knick-knacks.

"I'm coming. Yes, I found what I was looking for!" said Hank. He then loaded his arms with a fifties-style desk lamp and turned his flashlight towards the stairs.

"C'mon, Uncle Hank," said Darcy impatiently.

"I'm coming. I'm coming," said Hank as he quickly aimed the beam over to his stash. It looked all right. He then hustled up the dingy staircase.

Geraldine's fingertips danced nervously on the window ledge. Would she ever like to get her hands on Lizzie! For two days now, she had camped out in this widow's peak, staring out these darn windows! She had even thrown a blanket around herself and closeted herself up here, the source of heat and light being the flicker of her cigarettes and a worn-down candle. At times, she wondered about her sanity. Why was she playing stakeout chief? Had she lost her mind? But she knew the neighborhood had some strange happenings, and Lizzie did too. Good old crazy Lizzie; that woman knew something. Lizzie been over to Hank's place at least four times, maybe more. Those were the times she had noticed. What she would give to be able to get near that house!

Geraldine awkwardly moved about the dwarfed space cluttered with the accumulation of trash. Popcorn, sesame seed bagel pieces, and peanut shells were everywhere, like some kid with a baseball cap had settled in for a ball game. That kid was her, but she abhorred this ugly mess. At that moment, all she cared about was what was outside her window. She eased her Colonial rocker closer to the window and clumsily knocked over a pile of books. One rather large volume fell to her side and sloppily opened to the middle pages. It was getting later in the day, but there was enough light to accent the contents. Indeed, what she needed was a tattered memento book of long ago. She used to do that kind of thing, collect pictures and memorabilia of her life, all those good times. As she paged through, she was awed by the places she had been—San Francisco, Italy, the Hawaiian Islands—and the activities she had found fulfilling. Indeed, it was like looking at a life of a famous magazine personality. Yet the woman who filled these pages only remotely looked like her. Geraldine paused. The furrows of skin between her eyes deepened. There she was, arm in arm with dear Stanley, the man she had once loved. She brought the picture closer to her nose, which twitched in disgust at the repugnant blend of molds from the many months of dust and decay. Stanley was dressed so fine in his silk pinstriped suit. After all, he had been a big shot at the First National Bank. She remembered that day; she had had the day off from the same bank, so, in her summer attire of clam diggers and a peasant blouse, she had paid him a visit. She giggled. She had to admit they made an odd-looking pair, but she also knew heads would often turn for a second look, and they weren't interested in Stanley. Geraldine stared more intensely at another photograph that still showed color. Who were these strange men in the background? They were laughing as they lifted pieces of fabric and whirled them about, with their bright colors that boasted shapes of Halloween costumes.

A loud rumble of a worn truck engine went down the narrow, snow-plowed street. Oh yes, Hank was back. Geraldine arched her back to watch, sliding the album to her side. Her view of that far down the street was obscured by tree limb and snow bank, but Geraldine perched a strong pair of binoculars on her nose and hoped for the best. She moved this way and that, trying to get a decent view. Why, that Hank. Two young women were moving about the truck, and they were pulling something out from the truck bed. The two women moved several cardboard boxes that appeared rather heavy. The woman in the red woolen cap had struggled to steady herself, and the other woman had come to her rescue. Geraldine squinted into the binoculars. That one in the red cap reminded her of someone; who was it? She paused and closed her eyes. *Now, Geraldine, just think. The hat, the dark coat, and the slight figure.* Oh, yes, now she remembered. Of course. It was Joliana from a couple houses down on the other side. Geraldine's eyes opened wide. What would Joliana be doing at Hank's? Why, the Stallers and the Williards had loathed each other for years, although at one time they seemed to get along, about twenty years ago. That was about the time her wonderful Stanley was killed in an auto accident and her dog disappeared. About that time, she had lost her grip on reality. Geraldine refocused the binoculars on the two women. She tried looking this way and that, but to her dismay, the women and the truck were gone.

Hank chuckled and chomped nosily on a stolen candy bar as he surveyed the loot his niece and her accomplice had accumulated in a couple of hours. Not bad, not bad at all. He walked around the piles that filled every available spot in the kitchen and den area. He noted clothing, lawn equipment, expensive luggage, and even some frivolous items, like perfume, more chocolate bars, and jellybeans. Hank then glanced out the front window. The remainder of the bar and its wrapper slid to the floor as Hank rushed out the back door, nearly tripping Darcy.

"Hey, watch it! Where are you going? The least you could do is help me with this box. You asked for this stuff!" said Darcy angrily.

"Darcy, Darcy come here!" said Bette.

"I'm coming. Can't you see here I've got my hands full? A little help please!"

"Darcy, now!"

Darcy looked about the clutter of antique stuff and the spanking new merchandise attempting to find an empty space. Finally, she put the large carton down, allowing her cramped arms to find relief. Darcy threw her coat open. Even though it was barely twenty degrees out there, all this hustling about was making her sweaty.

"C'mon, Darcy, you'll miss this!"

Darcy ambled through the piles of loot to the dingy, linen-framed living room window.

Now she knew why Bette was so anxious. There was Hank, outside, with a police car resplendent with lights flickering and a full-fledged police officer. Great. Just great. Hank was fully animated, like a cartoon character gone wild. His arms were flailing about, and he was doing a kind of foot-stomping dance.

"Dar, should we stick all this stuff somewhere else?" said Bette, her voice tight.

"I should say so. No, wait … look, something's happening."

Both women stared out the picture window like it was a show at the cinema.

"Uncle Hank seems to be less angry."

"Yeah, now he's talking calmly to that guy, and it even looks like they're laughing," said Bette.

"Yeah."

Hank removed an item from his pocket and gave it to the officer. Then the long-haired policeman handed Hank something metallic that gleamed in a ray of sun. Darcy squinted. It was shiny, like chocolate bar wrappers, but it was definitely not one of those. Instead, it was an unidentified package. Her curiosity was over the top.

Hank burst into the kitchen, his normally ruddy complexion intensified by the snow and ice.

"Uncle Hank, what was that all about?" asked the women in unison, almost knocking Hank over.

Hank sternly eyed the girls and wiped the mucous from his nose with his hand.

"Does he know about us?"

"Why were you yelling and then laughing?"

Hank brushed by the girls and grabbed his thick espresso-like coffee, which had now thoroughly cooled.

"He knows."

"He knows what?"

"That cop, his name is Jerry. He said he saw you two at Marty's."

"He did? But how?" asked Bette.

"Right. There weren't any police there that day. It was pretty quiet," added Darcy.

"No, he didn't see you personally, but it's here, all here," said Hank as he tossed a video tape on the table. "It's a copy and a bit grainy, but it's all there."

"The cameras ... but I thought we had smashed them good. We had even gone to that store at about supper time that day so that we wouldn't miss anything," recoiled Bette.

"Well, you didn't do so good on one of them. It caught you two red-handed."

"But how did he know who we are and where we were?"

"As I told you before, this street has eyes and ears," said Hank.

"But why didn't he arrest us?" said Bette.

"Because, he didn't ... and he won't," said Hank as he hustled to the basement door. "Look, I've got some things to do. Please don't bother me," said Uncle Hank as his snow-covered shoes slipped puddles behind him.

"But, Uncle Hank ..." said Darcy.

"Please, stay and talk to us," pleaded Bette.

No answer.

Both women rushed to the basement door and tugged at the handle. It was no use. Uncle Hank had locked himself in from the other side. Bette took the tape and turned it this way and that and then walked it over to the antiquated television. Her head shook back and forth, and her mouth quivered as she looked helplessly at Darcy. "Your Uncle Hank doesn't own a VCR, so how are we supposed to see this?"

"I really don't know, but I wish I could just march that tape over to Sarah's house, since she owns all the most recent electronics."

"Sarah's place? But doesn't she live in Upstate New York, like hours from here?" said Bette.

"Yeah. But I can wish, can't I? Now I just have to wait on Hank, and I hate waiting on people. You know that I like working things out for myself, and now I have all these complications."

"But it was your idea to come here, or don't you remember? Heck, I wouldn't mind if we just jumped into our car and got the hell out of here." Bette stared intently at Darcy.

Darcy tried to avert her friend's hardened look, her cheekbones and eyebrows arched. She really didn't like when Bette got like this. "We will leave when we finish, I promise!"

Bette shrugged, headed into the kitchen, and threw open the refrigerator.

Chapter Twelve

"What on earth are you doing?" asked Tony. Confusion shadowed his usually playful disposition.

"Oh, um, I'm putting away groceries."

"Putting away? It looks like you've been taking everything out! There's stuff everywhere in this kitchen!" said a disgruntled Tony as he negotiated his way through the piles.

"Well, I just went shopping for Dad and for us. Dad's stuff, which is mostly canned goods, is still in the car. I'm trying to finish ours first."

"Yeah, you've been finishing, all right. Just look at this place! You're always so particular about things. Everything is supposed to be spotless. Why, you often take my supper dish before I'm finished and wash it!"

"Sorry, I was just looking for something. I'll clean up right away."

"Well, you had better. This place is a disaster scene!"

"So then maybe you're the one who needs order," said Joliana, her voice a sharp whisper. She looked over at her husband, who was thoroughly confused. He was so angry. What would he say if he knew why she had destroyed the kitchen, that she had lost, really lost, two important cards? He would certainly have a fit then. He would be all over her case. But she really should say something.

"Hon," Joliana said softly so she could establish a peaceful playing field.

"And where were you last night?" interrupted Tony. "And how come you're not at work? One reason why I came home is that Tom told me you had called in sick. He said you sounded pretty bad."

Joliana unloaded the final armful of groceries on the only bare spot left on the table. She smiled tensely, attempting to cajole her husband. "C'mon, let me brew up your favorite coffee, and we'll have a chat."

Moments later, they both sat in the fastidiously tidy den, the one room Joliana had not dismantled. It was their TV viewing room. She preferred to read, so she hardly spent time there. The story of the last twenty-four hours came in halting sentences from her lips—that is, most of it.

"So that's why you came home so late?"

"Yes."

"Well, why didn't you tell me? You know I'm here for you," said Tony, his arched eyebrow matching his displeasure.

"I thought you would be mad at me, that you would think less of me."

"Now, Joliana, I have to say that this news is not a cause for celebration, but we'll work it out."

"I know," said Joliana as her trembling hand attempted to lift her cup of flavored brew. It was cold.

"Well, we need to get working on this."

"I know."

"Okay then, I'll call the store and have Marty tear the place apart for the cards."

"Okay. And I'll keep looking around here."

"Yeah, I guess so. We'll look together, and I'll help you fix everything up again."

"And if we don't find them?" said Joliana, looking directly at her husband.

"Then we start making phone calls."

"Phone calls?"

"Yes," said Tony resolutely, "we will need to cancel your credit card and pay a visit to the Motor Vehicle Department."

"Do you really think someone could have used the card already and rung up a bill?"

"Why not? It's a major credit card, with a high ceiling. Someone could be having a party."

"Well, wouldn't we know that already, I mean, if a lot of purchases were made …"

"Jo," began Tony, using her nickname in his most gentle voice, "you believe you lost it yesterday, so it may take some time for the transactions to register and get to us. But I'll talk to Marty and see if we can find some shortcuts."

"And what if the worst happens and they charge things to the very limit?"

"Then we'd deal with it," said Tony firmly. "We'll figure our way out."

"So we'll be okay?" said Joliana, feeling relieved with her husband's take-charge attitude.

"I guess so," said Tony.

"What? Guess so? You knew so a few moments ago! What is it?"

"Well, isn't there more to the story? Like you didn't visit your cousin last night; instead you went to Marty's store."

Joliana could feel her face redden. It began at her widow's peak and traveled down her neck. She was candy apple red.

"I'm sorry, hon. I kind of forgot that part."

"How am I supposed to help you if you don't tell me everything? I'm your husband. You can trust me."

"But, Tony, how did you know?"

"Jerry, from the county police. He and his buddies stopped by the mart today. Jerry said he saw you, but that you took off so fast he couldn't catch you."

"Oh?"

"Said he had stopped by to check the place."

Now it was Joliana's turn to be confused. Who was this Jerry, and why had he said he followed her? As far as she knew, he hadn't. Why did he lie?

Tony reached into his pocket and pulled out a good-sized chocolate bar and broke off a piece.

"Want a piece?"

Joliana was dumbfounded. Her husband was munching on the confection that, supposedly, the crooks had plundered.

"Hon, do you want a piece or not?"

"Tony, where did you get that bar?"

"Jerry, when he came by, offered one, so I accepted." He looked over at the defined arch in Joliana's carefully penciled eyebrow. "What? What is wrong?"

"Didn't you tell me Marty's was robbed of money and a load of candy bars—those candy bars?"

Tony's ambitious chewing slowed as he considered the ramifications of his wife's logic. Then he broke off another piece of the peanut-studded chocolate and shoved it into his mouth.

"It's nothing, Joliana. You're making too much of this," said Tony.

"I think there may be something …"

"Joliana," began Tony a bit more firmly, "let it go. It means nothing."

She shrugged and headed into the kitchen and rearranged her kitchen cupboard with her morning purchases.

Chapter Thirteen

Jepson Creek sloshed and twisted through the ample vegetation. Both deciduous leaf and weed dwelled together, as did fawn and feathered creatures of all sorts. They all enjoyed the warm embrace of the forested haven with the delicate light wind that would weave about and around the cedar and blackberry bush. While badger and beaver anchored their foundations to secure a long-term address, others heeded the call of this naturally pristine place, especially in the summer. They came in their simple T-shirts and faded, frayed dungarees; their shrieks of delight blended with their laughter and bellowing tones—wild-haired boys. They raced through the wooded area with abandon, snapping twigs, tripping on stray vines and angular rocks. They were all single-minded in pioneering through the jungle-like foliage. Soon they reached Jepson Creek. They ran alongside the merry crystal waterway as it bounced and swayed over rock and fallen debris. The boys then wasted no time as they waded in the shallow finger of the creek until it widened and pooled itself into a natural swimming hole. Their cries and cackles were then enmeshed in the splashing of aquatic play. Then would come the challenge of skipping stones; who would skip the most over the chortling stream? Good clean fun.

The boys did their own kind of pioneering in the shelter of the woods. They brought scythes and rudimentary tools fashioned by their own hands. Taking large branches that were sharpened to a clean edge, as well as stones that were naturally formed like ancient arrowheads, the three buddies set forth to clear a portion of the land to create a secret place. Utilizing all their resourcefulness, they secured plank upon plank with nails and a hammer, some from their family tool box. The threesome was ready to embark on its carpentry adventure. It was slow work, tedious and frustrating. But they remained undaunted. While school and family and rain and sleet gave ample opportunity for procrastination, they applied beaver-like focus whenever they could. Finally, the makeshift dwelling, that lay flush against a short hill, was ready. It resembled a life-size Lincoln log house, except every angle lacked perfection. It appeared to list a bit to the right, and there were many holes between the wooden beams, which lent view to the single room—the secret room. Creating a concoction of mud and straw and a bit of store-bought concrete, they patched every odd crack until the inside of the room was as dark as a bear's cave. Then they piled in old comforters and throw-away seat cushions, as well as candles and a bulging bag of flashlights and batteries. Now they could gather to sleep and eat and exchange ghastly tales together. All by themselves.

That was then. In the quest for progress, Jepson Creek diminished in its girth. This did not happen all at once, but each toddler step heralded the modern leather boot. It began with the sectioning off of the land to select families, who took the precious earth and transformed it into hay and corn as well as tomatoes and strawberries. The creek no longer ran through a natural habitat but instead aided the farmer in cultivating his crop. But as fall yielded to winter and spring to summer, bridges and concrete edifices made up of red brick and wood sprouted everywhere. Gone was the ample oak and hemlock. Gone was the gentle breeze that flowed through the forest, gently blowing a rippled design on the creek's face. A before and after picture would see land stripping at its best, a coal miner's delight but of incredible dismay to the young. Modern life, with all its ranch houses and factories, super food marts and libraries, had pitched its tent and was not going away. The creek, bit by bit, lessened its expanse until it became a mere trickle. The harsh drought of a decade before dried its furrowed fingers until all that was left was a sloping indentation in the ground floor. But a sign remained near the evaporated playground: Windslow Street.

All was not gone. A bit of childhood memory remained. Somehow, the bulldozing contractors had missed a small section of natural setting. While its planks of pressboard were sodden, moldy, and worn out in spots, and its makeshift roof was composed of discarded floor tiles and banged-up aluminum Christmas trees, the tiny structure was still standing. It had been the pride and joy of those prancing boys, a place to mellow out and share their innermost dreams as well as their fears played out in horrific storytelling. Sometimes the scary details left them with spiked hair and one eye wide open, cautious and watching. Indeed, its very location in the shadow of the Colonial homes of Old Wethersfield only lent more material to their ghostly tales, prompting goose bumps and chattering teeth.

The tiny dwelling would have been swallowed by its woodsy surroundings if it wasn't for the arrival of nail-bitten fingers and high adrenaline—the new round of neighborhood boys. They had appeared with their hammers and assorted wood planks, ready to settle into the hut with their boisterous tales and mysterious secrets. The tradition had been passed on.

Chapter Fourteen

Hank had finally come up from the basement, and the trio went out to, as Hank had put it, get the nets ready to catch a tiger. He and Darcy were chattering like excited geese that had just found a half-eaten McDonald's sandwich. Bette sat, arms crossed about her chest, a dour smirk thinning her ample lips. All this talk about a tiger ... she knew she was the bait and that this trip was no little joy ride. Uncle Hank and Darcy were planning something else with her at the front lines and it was making her crazy. She hunkered down in the back seat. She was so sick of being the sitting duck perched on the shopping post, just waiting to be picked off.

"Hey, Bette, how about we stop and get us a real down-home dinner, something juicy like a barbecued steak?" asked Hank. "I'm starved."

"Not hungry."

"C'mon, woman, get with the picture. Just a big one to pull off tomorrow and then we'll be sitting pretty—that is unless you would like to do more today?"

Darcy snickered.

Bette glared at both of them. "Leave me alone."

"Bette, you did a great job this morning," said Darcy. "Now to get you really looking like Joliana, with a little lipstick and hair color."

"Another heist? This morning was enough. You two are awfully greedy."

"Today was just small potatoes," said Hank. "Tomorrow will be the great Williard-Faracelli caper, opening an account in that woman's name."

"Hank, don't you think that is going too far? I mean, not the hit, but starting a new account. Why, we've already created a pretty good paper trail

…" Bette paused to gather her thoughts. "And don't you think that we're pushing our luck by using that woman's name again?" added Bette.

Hank's head violently shook back and forth. The aromatic scent of his Borkum-Riff-filled pipe swayed with him as he puffed harder. "You two just shut up! Were making a stop in the morning at the Valley Electronics Store to pick us up a few pieces of the state-of-the-art entertainment world, and that's that." The smoke from his pipe now encircled him and filled the entire car.

Darcy's eyes brightened. "You mean we could get us a fancy computer system and maybe a nice big color television?"

"Yep, and maybe a nice VCR for you both to take back to PA and watch Bonnie and Clyde movies. And, of course, one for me, so we can watch that blasted tape from the mart."

"But why do we have to open a new account? Can't we just charge everything again like we did this morning?" persisted Bette.

Darcy's face twisted in frustration as she shot Bette a hostile "shut up" look. Bette would not be dissuaded; instead, she glared hard into the rearview mirror.

Hank returned her scowl in the overhead mirror. "We'll cross that bridge once we get there. Right now, let's stop and get that hair junk for Bette so she can get dolled up like Joliana."

Hank then drove into the drug store lot and parked.

"Hey, I remember this place," said Darcy. "I used to come here when I was a kid—you know Uncle Hank, when I used to live with you …" Her voice trailed off.

"Well, that's great, because you've been nominated to go in," Hank stated firmly.

"But why can't I go? After all, it's my makeover. I would like to pick out my own hair color and cosmetics."

Hank did not answer. Instead, he pulled the smoking tobacco from his pocket and stuffed his pipe.

"But what about me? Won't someone recognize me? I mean, I used to be a regular in this store," said Darcy.

Hank puffed silently for a long moment and then thrust his hand down into the crevasse of the torn seat. He rooted about and then his bulky, calloused fingers snatched up a dirty woolen cap that had probably been a bright orange at one time. He took the pilled and matted hat and threw it at Darcy.

Darcy's mouth fell open like the wooden doll in the ventriloquist's lap. Deciding against a retort, she then pursed her lips together and yanked hard at her shoulder-length ebony hair and twisted it into a makeshift bun. She hastily shoved the ugly cap tightly over her head. She threw open the truck door, its rusting hinges squealing in protest.

"Hey, you don't have to be such a sour puss about this," chided Hank as he rolled down the driver's window and watched Darcy.

"Darcy, please remember to get conditioner and an eyebrow pencil," added Bette.

Darcy ignored the prattle of her two cohorts as she hopped out of the truck and hurried to the store.

It was like she had never left. Darcy milled about the drug store, noting some minor renovations, like various newfangled cardboard end displays, but it was pretty much as she had remembered it. Fifties-style design permeated the place, with its dim lighting and a thick layer of dust on everything. The smell of burnt toast and brewing coffee meant that the cozy luncheonette was still operating in the back of the store. Gosh, with all these scents and sights, she could recall the last thought she had had almost twenty years before. She had been with a couple of friends, or what she had naively believed to be friends. They were hanging out at the food counter, twirling and fidgeting in their swivel seats as they ordered their usual hamburger and fries. They were just getting their order when she heard conversation in a side aisle. She wasn't supposed to have been privy to this discussion, but she was well within earshot.

"Hey, Jen, are you meeting Darcy here?" asked Lisa.

"Yep, but I'd rather be somewhere else."

"Why is that?"

"You do know that Darcy lives with that awful uncle of hers and that she's got no other family."

"So?"

"Well, she had told me that she was raised in West Hartford, near the county club, but she lied to me. I heard she was in an orphanage and was involved in a lot of criminal activity and maybe even went to prison."

"Prison? Gosh, Jen, I didn't know these things. So do you think she's dangerous?"

"Of course. You realize that those kinds of people are total losers, and anyone who hangs out with them is scum as well."

Lisa's ruddy complexion paled. "Jen, I just remembered that I have to be home today to baby sit my little sister," she said, rushing out of the store.

The ketchup-covered crispy fry hung limp, making it only halfway to Darcy's mouth. Then, in one flick of the wrist, the long fry sailed across the counter, barely missing Jen. Darcy then turned on her stool to confront this traitor of a friend. It did not go well. Within moments, alliances were formed as her eating companions joined with Jen. Voices escalated and hair was pulled as ketchup was smeared on faces and the remains of lunch went flying about. Mr. Post, the owner, intervened, and the outcome was not good. Darcy had been banned from these premises while her friends were not given any correction. So much for loyalty.

Darcy rubbed her hands on her slacks since they had become clammy and shaky. Such hostilities had happened so long ago, but the prickly feeling in her spine and the throbbing in her heart was very much real. A wave of melancholy washed over her, and the toughed-skinned, mouthy Darcy could sense a well of tears pinching her eyes. With the sleeve of her coat, she quickly brushed them away. *Get a grip, girl.*

She walked down the aisle where all the hair products were stocked and looked hard at to the offerings. She wanted Bette's hair to resemble Joliana's corn-colored locks and not turn out looking a weird green or something worse. Now Bette was a dirty blonde, so it shouldn't be so difficult to just lighten her hair a couple of shades. However, to be on the safe side, Darcy chose two color types; she could mix them if she had to. Her eyes landed on the label titled "Decadent chocolate." Her color. Even though she had never done her hair around Bette, maybe it was time for her to have a touch-up as well. Darcy snickered. How ironic; here she was, buying the blonde treatment for her friend, while she preferred every root to be extremely dark.

Why?

Darcy mused. She knew why. Her transformation had been swift. Just a mere two weeks after her encounter in the drugstore, she had taken on a new persona. She had become gloomy and grim on the inside, and her external effects matched. Deep blues, sepias, and black adorned her model-like figure in an assortment of shirts, jeans, and socks. She topped it all off with a shiny, ebony leather coat, matching boots, and sometimes a smear of black lipstick. Gazing in the long bathroom mirror, she admired the tough-as-nails exterior, the unblinking stare, and arched cheekbones that at times appeared sinister. Gothic she was. And Darcy had often heard the street term whispered behind her back.

To hell with all of them. Darcy let out a sigh. Yes, it was true: she had been a forsaken waif at the Davenport Street Home for girls. And it was also true that some petty shoplifting flings had put her before the state troopers, but she hadn't been all that bad. She had tried to be a decent human being when she lived with her uncle, although she had told a white lie or two. But that falling out with those so-called friends was like a match being lit to a firecracker. She had gone ballistic, packed her bags, and left Uncle Hank's house. Darcy hitched to the city of New York and established herself as an ace pickpocket. Word got out quickly on the street that she was able to commandeer her own fleet of long, sticky fingers. Then she met Bette at a hamburger joint one day, and they became perfect partners in crime. It had been a golden time, but now Bette was wavering. It was all Hank's fault. He was putting too much pressure on them. But, actually, it was really her fault since she had come to this town. She would just have to make it up to Bette somehow. Darcy approached the counter and dumped her pile of hair color and sweep of Maybelline items, throwing in a few candy bars. She would do her best to work this all out.

Chapter Fifteen

Pete kept looking over his shoulder as he trudged through the snow. He had stayed off the major turnpikes; the sloppy back roads and yards gave him ample cover and he likened himself to those many furry creatures: swift and tenacious. However, his makeshift foot gear of well-worn sneakers with gashes on both sides was no match for all this arctic pile-up. Neither was his thin, almost threadbare jacket. Pete paused and looked up. The cerulean of the sky provided the perfect background for the dancing array of barren branches. It was picture-postcard perfect. Pete drew in a deep breath. He had forgotten—or had he ever noticed?—how invigorating nature could be. Yet now was not the time. The sun was shining, but he felt like his toes and fingers were numbed enough to become frostbitten. He smirked. He was finally out of that hell hole, rotten cement cell, only to find himself turning into that rock hard turkey he had seen in the prison's huge freezer. Turkey! Yes, that was what he was! He had been the fall guy! After all, he had spent all those years in prison, and what had been his crime? They said it was bank robbery and murder. Why, he hadn't really intended to hurt anyone. That teller had just been in the way. Hell, the authorities had no gun or stolen goods, but they pinned everything on him, anyway. Lucky him.

So he had been locked up based on a bank full of eyewitnesses. He had been at the wrong place at the wrong time. All those dumb lawyers had was a portion of his Superman suit and a whole lot of made-up stuff. Heck, the truth would have made better press.

Pete reached the clearing and squinted, with his left hand shielding his eyes. Yep, he was almost there. All he had to do was follow Jepson Creek or what was left of it. He saw the indentation of land where it had been; all signs of water had evaporated and not even an ice crystal remained. So much for the good times at the creek, of days in his youth when jumping in that water was so invigorating. It was like another lifetime ago. Pete turned right and looked up at the sign. Winslow Street. The sign seemed to grow from a mound of dirty snow and ice. Yep, he was almost there. He had to collect some things that were properly his and then put a lot of space between him and this part of the country, maybe every skip off to Canada or Mexico. The latter would be just fine, where the air would be warm and toasty and he could kick back.

Where should he start? He looked over at the old-fashioned white bungalow in need of a paint brush and a strong arm.

Old Joe Williard's house. Yeah, he had been good ol' Joe until he bailed. Left him and Hank, just like that, and you know what it was he said? That he had a wife and children he didn't want to implicate! Pete chuckled cruelly. He should have thought about that before he started. Boy, he would like to give that guy a piece of his mind. Pete stared hard at the farm house. His right hand tugged at his straggly beard almost in hope of improving the growth, but he always did this when he was thinking. His fiery beard matched his matted curls, giving him a mean look. Yes, he realized that he was small but he was quite mighty. In the joint, he had worked out big time, both in the makeshift gym and in the everyday filthy jobs, like highway clean-up and moving rocks. They also had him digging holes and moving heavy boxes. But it had all paid off. He was strong in body, strong in mind. And now this wonderful opportunity had floated down like a golden ticket. Freedom.

Pete pulled his collar up a bit around his neck, the nip of the wind biting through his thin jacket and even thinner pants. Prison clothes. Definitely a neon light.

Pete ducked behind an evergreen tree and looked around. Soon the neighborhood kids would come home from school and possibly initiate some snowball fights. So he had better tend to things. Pete quickly edged to the back door of the house. He shook the handle and the door opened with ease. Pete smiled. It was a good thing that Joe was cheap and hadn't replaced the worn lock. He was in, and moments later, he found his way to the musty attached garage. This was the key storage spot since some of the period homes had no basement. Everything was in piles everywhere, a pasty white dust covering it all. Gosh, Joe had become a sloppy pack rat. He could feel his facial muscles tighten into a long grimace. He had no idea where to look, but he would give it a try.

He tugged on the cord of the overhead lighting and began his search. At first, he tried to be quiet and a bit more deliberate in his actions. But his impatience gave way. He trashed box after box, tossing them about with his hulk-like arms. What he was looking for was not there, but he found a sort of consolation prize when he found some street clothing. Pete quickly shed his prison skin and threw on Joe's old stuff. He chuckled as he attempted to secure the pants and shirt that had fit a more ample man. Indeed, he looked ready to do a stint as a hired hand at the Barnum and Bailey Circus, but anything was better than that awful prison attire. Pete turned around. The gleam of metal glittered like a rare diamond. "What the hell!"

"Hello, Pete, I've been expecting you."

"Expecting me?"

"Yeah, your breakout is all over the news."

"I figured."

"And while it would be in your best interest to get away from here, you chose to return to little ol' Windslow Street."

"Yeah, how about that?" said Pete.

"I see you've helped yourself to my rummage sale stuff, which could use a bit of alteration."

"Well, at least I look better than you, even in this stupid clothing. Look at you; you've become pudgy and gray, a rather unjolly old man!"

Joe self-consciously scratched a balding spot on the side of his head. Ever since his wife had died, he had eaten all wrong. He did not like to cook, so whatever he could grab that was tasty and easy, he gulped down, or he would feast at Joliana's. He knew he had added inches to his favorite jeans and they refused to zip. And exercise, well that went with the end of his corn crops. But Pete had no right to speak to him like that. "So what of it, Pete? Maybe you're in decent shape, but at least I'm not in trouble with the law."

"Yeah, and why is that? It's because you're yeller, that's why. Leaving everything to Hank and I while you go crawling home to your mama."

"Shut up! I did my part, planned the heist, and came up with the clever idea of the costumes."

"Costumes that you pawned off on your old lady to do, and I've often wondered why she made them and if she had any idea what they were for. She must have known something was up."

"Hey, leave her out of it. Let the poor woman rest in peace," said Joe.

"So the old lady is dead, and those daughters you whined about are probably all gone too. Everyone's gone and deserted you."

"Like I said, Pete, leave my family out of this."

"But they were the reason that you bailed. You ran off like a scared raccoon."

"That's the way it was, Pete. I'm not saying that I regret anything. I did what I had to do". Joe paused and glared at Pete. "So what do you care about my business? You mean nothing to me, nothing!" Joe brandished the Smith & Wesson above his head.

"Hey, that's my gun!" said Pete.

"Dare you to come and get it!"

Pete lunged at Joe. The strength of the muscled midget took the ailing seventy-year-old Joe off guard. At one moment, the gun was aimed, dead accurate, at Pete, and the next second, the weapon hurled in a rocket-like trajectory as Pete kicked Joe in his abdomen—hard. Joe grabbed his gut, tightened with pain, and fell into three stacked grates, which produced a domino effect on everything around him. Then an intense blast shook the room as the contents of the Smith & Wesson discharged. Then all that could be heard was the rhythmic pumping of the antiquated oil burner.

Chapter Sixteen

"What the hell are you doing?" screamed Bette as Darcy plunged her head into the peeling, foul-smelling sink.

"Gotta get all this crap out of your hair."

"Ow! My eyes are burning and my scalp is on fire! Darcy, you're killing me!" said Bette, now certain of her friend's ineptitude.

"Stop being such a baby and let me finish this. I have to get your hair as clean as possible before I shampoo and condition it."

"Let me up. I've got to wipe my eyes, now!" Bette yanked herself away from this wannabe beautician and grabbed the nearest towel. She rubbed her eyes and then her head.

"Darn you, Darcy; even my sweatshirt is sopping wet! Can't you do anything right?"

"Will you shut up! You know, Bette, even though your head is still wet, I believe the color took pretty well. When Hank gets back, he'll just love the new you."

"Yeah, let me see in the mirror."

"It's right in front of you."

"Yeah, right. My hair is still awfully dark, isn't it?"

"It's just wet. You'll be a raging blonde any minute now—that is, if you would just let me finish."

Darcy prompted Bette back to the sink and then she quickly piled on the shampoo and the two applications of conditioner. Bette squirmed and hurled a rainbow of rude remarks at Darcy, but she paid no attention. Then she found a dry towel and scrubbed until the hair was damp and somewhat fluffy.

"Too bad we don't have a hair dryer. Now you're pulling out my hair!"

"All right, all right. Calm down. You're acting like it's the end of the world or something. Let's put you by the warm radiator so you can completely dry."

"Hey, Darcy, how do you know about hair dye anyway?"

"Well, I'm surprised that you didn't ask me that before." Darcy eyed her friend with amusement, but Bette's body language was fiercely serious. "Well, it's just that I've had my share of color changes. I wasn't always this midnight black. I've been red, blonde, and even blue."

"I guess that you had a different life before you met me."

"Perhaps. I always been into trying new things, and you're definitely one of them."

"What do your mean by that?"

"All this adventure we've had off the beaten path; you know, our Bonnie and Clyde stint. And now Uncle Hank has added an interesting dimension, a bit of impersonation and higher-stake crime. We've moved into the big leagues!"

The darker arches of her eyebrows contrasted with the blonde ringlets. "You mean that this thing with Joliana is getting more complicated. I mean, we spent all that money," said Bette.

"Bette, you are so naïve. We are changing you to look more like Joliana and you think that we're done? Why, we have only just begun!"

Bette hung her head awkwardly. The color of candied apples flowed rapidly from her neck to her cheek and complimented the blonde highlights. "It's just that we always seem to do what you want. I didn't want to come to this blasted state, Connecticut, no less! And I never figured we would become such criminals. It was all fun for a while, but now we could get in some real trouble."

"Bette, believe it or not, we're already in a heaping load of trouble. Once we finish this stint, we'll have to put a lot of distance between us and this place."

"How about we take off now? I'll go grab my things."

Darcy intercepted Bette as she began to collect her belongings. Pulling at Bette's oversized maroon sweater, which hung limply over her shoulder, Darcy curtly directed, "Do it or else!"

"Take your hands of me, you, you tyrant! Both you and your uncle can both rot in a damn cell one day, but not me!" Bette abruptly turned to leave the fifties-style peeling kitchen for good. How dare they treat her like that! All she had done for Darcy, all she had risked! For what? She had no permanent address, no formal schooling. She had barely passed the GED exam to get her high school diploma. She was not connected with family since her mother had died and her father had taken off to who knows where. As for romantic inclinations, there hadn't been anyone for many years. She just didn't have the right look. Besides, when you're doing the Bonnie and Clyde thing, there isn't much time for a relationship, only drinking Singapore slings and having hollow chats at a nearby pub. Indeed, all she had was Darcy. This woman had become everything to her: family, work associate, and friend. Darcy had been there when no one else had taken notice of her; she had been there to rescue her, direct her, and be her support and guide. Bette sighed. She both loved and hated Darcy. She had become too dependent and was losing herself. She was becoming a walking, breathing extension of Darcy. But she figured this much: all the small scams they had pulled off had not hurt anyone, not really. Oh, yes, they had taken money and things, but never like this. This time they were hurting someone for real, and this person had a name and a face. A face she would never forget! Bette grabbed the handle of the door. By God, she was out here!

With the stealth of a sly cougar, Hank eased himself between the door and Bette. For a moment, inky pools of lava raged in his eyes; then, suddenly, a certain light danced in them, taking on a sense of mirth. Bette had flinched, fully expecting a fist to her face, but instead, Hank's demeanor had changed. He was laughing!

"So just where do you think you're going? Bette, we have so much to do. We have to get you ready to play your role. We need to get you dressed just so and make sure your forged handwriting will get by. Now, please move away from the door. I have something for you."

Under his arm, he carried a large brown bag that oozed delectable smells of chicken and beef and rice. An early suppertime.

"Time to party!" exclaimed Hank as he cleared the old-fashioned trestle table, pushing greasy condiments to one side and plopping the oily bag in the middle. "Let's eat!"

Bette stared indignantly at Darcy. Darcy avoided her friend and busied herself by quickly throwing paper plates and forks on the table. "Uncle Hank, that was so nice of you to buy supper. I'm so hungry I could eat some of that moldy stuff you've got in your fridge."

Hank chuckled. "Now that would be a crazy thing to do, but eat up so we have the strength for tomorrow morning. I would like to leave early. Hey Bette, why are you just standing there with your hair all wet? Sit down and eat before Darcy and I devour it all!"

Bette hesitantly walked over to table. Hank was swiftly opening the goodly-sized boxes of steaming Asian food. The medley of smells burst forth: the freshness of Chinese vegetables, the savory beef and chicken, and the perfect, pungent sauces. Goodness, she was hungry. She hadn't realized just how empty her stomach had become. All three charged the table and built their plates like Egyptian pyramids; the rice anchored the meat and veggies, and the fancy mushroom decorated the peak. Conversation was slow to start, but each forkful appeased the angry beast each one of them had hiding inside.

"Even with Chinese cabbage hanging from your mouth, you look quite pretty, Bette." Hank rose from his seat, wiping the drippings from his mouth on his shirt sleeve. He went into the bathroom and rummaged about and returned carrying a shiny implement. He waved it in front of Bette. "Now all we have to do is get the right hairstyle."

The egg roll fell to the table as Bette's eyes grew wide like those of deer caught in a headlight.

Darcy swiftly took the scissors from her uncle and patted Bette on the shoulder. "Now before you get all crazy here, I think that uncle is right; you do need a bit of a shaping. Now I can do this for you if you just sit still …"

"C'mon, you guys. You buy me clothes like Joliana's, you find makeup, you color my hair, and now you're going to cut it!" Bette waved her hands over her head in rebellion.

"Bette, it's like I was saying before: we have to finish this thing. Just one more little caper and we will be done," cajoled Darcy.

"Yeah, you had better or else!" demanded Hank.

"Or else what, Hank? You're going hurt me or turn me in or …"

"Shut up, you two. We're all in this together and we plan to stand by our word. Right, Hank?" Darcy stared hard into her friend's lovely emerald eyes. She was speaking to such an unsettled heart. "It's okay, Bette, it really is."

Bette's demeanor softened. "Darcy, you said this will be it; once we finish here, we start something else, and I mean something that will keep us out of jail."

"Okay, Bette, now just let me cut you hair."

"Promise?"

"Promise," said Darcy with the genuine voice of a would-be politician.

Bette grabbed the kitchen chair and pulled it from the table. Then she wrapped her neck in the damp towel she had just used to dry her hair. "I'm ready."

Darcy snipped and lifted Bette's hair, and cut at this angle and that. She fluffed her hair with a dry towel to remove the excess hair and give some volume. Then she took some eye shadow and a bit of blush and completed the look. Darcy then marched Bette to the bathroom mirror.

"Wow, I really look like her! I didn't know you could cut hair like this. You know, Darcy, once this is over, let's get us a beauty salon. It would be great fun."

Hank chuckled. "Yep, you're looking good. We just have to get …"

"Bette, you're so pretty, so very pretty." Darcy went on humming the popular tune of Maria in *West Side Story*, a play she remembered from high school.

"Yes, she's so very pretty," parroted Hank as he began pulling the recently purchased feminine apparel out of the bags. Darcy continued to hum the show tune, grabbing a lovely sweater. She waved it about herself like a cheerleader at a football game.

"Darcy, what are you doing? That's my stuff. I mean, some of it is the Joliana outfit but the rest is mine."

"C'mon, Bette, come and get them!"

Bette went after her. Darcy fell into Hank, who had also stepped into the action by wrapping a women's shirt around his middle and sticking a pair of lacey underwear on his head. Then he did a little dance that was a combination of the jitterbug and the twist.

"Uncle Hank, you're too much. Gosh, I didn't know you could be so much fun!" said Darcy.

"Ah, you didn't know I had it in me, I'm just full of surprises. Now help me get this crap off so we can dress Bette for her debut tomorrow."

Bette and Darcy hurried over to Hank and began to unshackle him from the confinement of his wardrobe. Despite Hank's verbal tirade, the two women laughed and hooted and sang themselves silly.

Chapter Seventeen

Walking always helped. Even though the paved road boasted icy patches here and there, Joliana had to get some fresh air. While she had only lost the two cards Monday night, it seemed like she had been on a fox hunt for months. She hadn't slept last night; she had had a wrestling match with the sheets and quilts, which were in a tight ball in the morning, It didn't help that Tony had retired in his easy chair and his evasion had only added to her guilt and confusion. But some of the glacier had melted with her candid discussion with Tony this morning. He said that he would contact all the necessary authorities today, such as the bank and identity theft bureaus. She was to make her own contacts, one being the Department of Motor Vehicles, since she was now driving without a license. Darn! She wasn't going there until she was absolutely certain the cards couldn't be found. So she searched every room, hoping that she had missed something. No such luck. Her mind was muddled; her eyes were sandy and blurry. She wanted to crawl back under the covers and forget the whole incident, but she knew she couldn't. Her nerves were frayed like the ancient wiring in her father's garage, and somehow her husband's willing hand was not helping the anxiety. Joliana had an awful sense of foreboding that all these phone calls were not going to fix. The Band-Aid was too small for this open wound.

The late afternoon sun was perched on marshmallow clouds dancing about in preparation for a colorful sunset. Joliana wasn't paying a bit of attention. She kept glancing over her shoulder like she was afraid someone was after her. What was wrong with her? Why was she so suspicious and paranoid? Somehow she felt the stares of a thousand eyes, and they were all noting every minute detail. Joliana righted her soft, woolen, red cap and drew the matching scarlet scarf around her neck. How silly! Who could be interested in her? The thieves, that's who. Maybe they were sitting in some house or car and were getting ready to pounce any time now. Just maybe.

She was giving herself the creeps she would feel when various versions of haunted house stories were exchanged. Her ears were now burning and were definitely irritated and hot to the touch. Indeed, Joliana's worries often seemed to seep out her ears.

"C'mon, let's get going!" said Bette impatiently.

"I thought you weren't so eager …" began Darcy.

"Will you girls shut up and get in the truck! All this cackling could wake the dead," growled Hank. "And, Bette, you should put a hat on that damp hair of yours."

"Wow, Uncle Hank, I didn't think you cared about things like that," said Darcy.

"Yeah, yeah, are you coming with me or not?" said Hank as he headed for the driver's seat.

Joliana ducked behind a tight cluster of a snow-capped brush. Hank was certainly busy these days; he hardly ever entertained anyone. Yet two women were visiting, and the one she had glimpsed, with the woolen hat, looked vaguely familiar. The blue pickup made its way down the street. Joliana ever so quietly moved the branches aside; she just had to get a better look at these women. She gasped. Only a few feet from her were a pair of inhabited mud-caked boots. Who was this? Had he seen her? She refused to even breathe, and she felt akin to a deep sea diver. The tattered leather boots then moved. They headed right for the old Staller bungalow.

What was this guy up to? Then the strange man abruptly turned and stomped towards the rear of the house. He knelt near one of the cellar windows, which was obscured from years of unruly vine and evergreen growth. Then he went over to the rusty cellar hatchway and yanked on the handle. Joliana squinted, the late afternoon rays blinding her. She couldn't see well, but this much she knew: this man was up to no good.

"Just what do you think you're doing?"

The shoulder of the man shook as if he had shrugged off an irate monkey. He had hardly expected such an interruption.

"Gosh, it's still daylight and it looks like you're trying to break in! Hey, I wouldn't do that. People live in this house." The slight woman dressed in a tattered robe and slippers anchored herself in the snow. She had on especially dark sunglasses so large they filled her entire face, with the exception of her smeared lips, which were curled into a ruby red sneer.

It was Lizzie.

Lizzie received no reply from the stranger. Instead, she shot question after question at him like an annoying young child in the grocery store. Lizzie just would not give up.

"Woman, would you please shut up!" Pete turned and faced Lizzie, all five feet of him. His muscular frame and the menacing manner in which his lip turned upward, almost touching his snorting nose, was most alarming. But not to Lizzie.

"I will not shut up, at least not until you tell me what is going on." Lizzie's tone was intensely combative. She edged closer to the stranger, her diminutive form in a frayed housecoat offering a fierce challenge.

"You are one crazy woman to answer back to me!" With one punch to the cheek, Pete knocked Lizzie to the ground. A brittle tree limb cracked. Pete paused and looked around. Joliana squatted closer to the icy ground and the camouflaging foliage. Had he seen her? The man made an awful grunting noise as he looked in her direction. Then, with an efficient, deliberated movement, he hoisted Lizzie over his shoulder. So effortless was his manner that she appeared to be light as an angel food cake, which could not be since she was out cold. The man, dressed in ill-fitting dark clothing, then disappeared down the cellar hatchway of the Staller house.

Joliana then eased herself up. The speed and stealth of her younger days returned. Every hormone in her body had been summoned. She had to get away! She was definitely on auto pilot, with her stallion blinders secured so that she focused straight ahead. That awful man would not catch her!

Finally, she was home. Joliana looked up at the peeling gray paint and chuckled. She was home all right, the childhood home where her dad still lived. Well, she was here. It was time to call the police.

"Dad, Dad, please open the door!" She had no patience with that surge of adrenaline still pulsating in her veins. No answer. *To heck with this.* Joliana dragged her heavy keychain out of pocket and let herself in.

The kitchen was in shambles. Condiments were turned over on the table and the contents of the cabinets had been strewn about the yellowing tile floor. The refrigerator door was open wide, and milk and orange juice cartons lay at odd angles, dripping their sweetened goodness in puddles. What had happened here? This mess went way beyond her dad's penchant for the laid back look. Why, she had just been here yesterday—it had been yesterday?—and things were not this bad. Joliana rushed to the other side of the room, and not a moment too soon. She flipped the top burner off, killing the blue flame that had licked the iron skillet, charring what was left of hashed brown potatoes.

A groan came from the short hall leading to the garage.

"Dad, is that you?"

Then there was another moan and a heightened level of angst.

She moved towards her father's voice. "Dad, are you all right?"

Joliana gasped.

Clothing had been thrown about and storage boxes emptied, filling the garage with everything from Christmas ornaments to canned goods. In the middle of it all, a mound of red plaid and polyester was moving. Joe. Joliana hurried to her father's side. "Dad, you're bleeding," she said as she stooped to assess the situation. A gash from the older man's left temple to his cheek continued to ooze precious blood. Joe's off-white under shirt was stained and wine-colored streaks were evidenced on his khaki pants.

"What is going on?" said Joliana, trying to maintain the calm bedside manner she had learned about in nursing school. Somehow, an actual situation was harder to deal with. Then she added, "Did you fall?"

Joe Williard waved his good arm at his daughter. "I'm fine; just give me a chance." The older man twisted and turned and, grabbing onto a solid wooden box, he sat up. His well-stretched sweater, which boasted many pulls, hung over his slacks. The pocket on the left side of his trousers had been torn at the corner. Joe sputtered and grunted as he finally righted his titanic body. The twilight years were not what everyone made them out to be.

Joliana stayed close and spotted her father, careful not to irritate him.

Joe nodded to his daughter. "Could you please get me a glass of water? Better yet, make it a gin and tonic."

"I'll get you the water and a few things to fix you up." Joliana hurried to the kitchen and loaded her arms with a warm dish towel, antiseptic, bandages, and, yes, a glass of water.

She would not validate his drinking problem even though a bit of gin might ease the pain a bit.

She had taken this stand long ago, but everyone, her mother, her cousins, and of course, her father, thought she was too reactive and that she had the problem. Ah, such messy family dynamics.

Her arms full of Florence Nightingale regalia, Joliana stepped over an overturned package of letters and documents. One of the yellowed papers had caught on her foot, and with her left hand, she awkwardly pulled it off. She wasn't going to read it; after all, these were her father's personal matters. But a moment of weakness, of curiosity, overtook her. She quickly scanned the professionally detailed page. She was utterly dumbfounded and wondered if her mind was making up things. She reviewed the title and it was indeed her birth certificate, yet it held data that went beyond her understanding; for in the darkened line addressing the name of the father was the name of a stranger. Her biological father was someone she had never met? Could this be possible?

"Where the hell are you!" shouted her father.

"I'm coming, I'm coming. I know that you're a bit upset, but I wasn't sure where some of these things were, especially since your kitchen is such a mess," said Joliana as she stuffed the certificate into her side pocket. She would dissect each word as soon as she could; then she would have a serious talk with her dad.

"Can't a man get any help around here? First you leave me with no dinner and then you leave me here bleeding."

"Oh, be quiet and let me tend to your head." Joliana washed the gash over her father's eye and cleaned his face and neck. Then, rolling up the tube of first aid cream that stubbornly would not release it contents, she retrieved a thumb-full and smeared it on the wound. Joe fretted and cursed as she went about her work, but she chose to not respond to him. He was being such an annoying child!

"Will you hurry up? You make such a big deal out of things!"

"Well it looks like it was only a flesh wound. You should be okay. You will just have to keep it clean." Joliana stepped back and admired her handiwork. Her short stint with nursing school had given her a little know-how. Then she grabbed the flashlight and waved it in front of her father's eyes.

"What are you doing now? I'm in no mood for stupid games."

"I'm just checking to see if you're eyes are dilating properly. Just give me a minute more … everything appears to be okay."

"Well that's good news. Now I can get about my day."

"Not so fast, Dad. Now tell me what exactly happened."

"Can I have my drink? This old hurt man is very thirsty—right now!"

Joliana handed the crystal drinking glass to her father.

"Yuck! This is only water and it's tepid. Couldn't you do better than that?"

"If you mean that you want me to quench your whisky palate, the answer is no!"

Joe hunched his shoulders and gave his daughter a wary look. He took a small sip and then sloshed the rest, resulting in a puddle on his shirt. Then he placed the glass on side table. "Look what you made me do!"

She would not be waylaid. "I still haven't heard what happened to your head and why this place is such a mess. I believe that you had a break-in or an altercation with someone. There are so many strange things going on. In fact, I just came from the Staller house, and Lizzie was in trouble. I think it's time to call the police." Joliana went on a determined hunt for the phone.

"No you don't. No police." Joe scrambled to the phone and held it tightly under his arm.

"Then tell me what happened."

"I lost my balance, that's all. You know that I'm not that good on my feet."

Joliana stood before her father. In a firm voice, she demanded, "Give me the phone."

Joe pulled back from his daughter.

The door crashed open.

The crystal glass slipped from Joe's hand.

Both daughter and father stared in amazement at the uninvited visitor.

It was Geraldine.

Chapter Eighteen

Joliana let out a deep sigh in the frosty air. Her breath seemed to freeze in midair, which ironically felt like her life right now. She was walking Geraldine home, and nightfall was quickly descending. Sloppy, dirty snow seeped between Geraldine's thin leather shoes as Joliana prodded the woman toward her home. What was this housebound woman doing outside? She hadn't left her home for about twenty years because she had that odd condition called agoraphobia, a fear of public places or leaving the comfortable ones. This situation was so bizarre. Some standup comedian out there would certainly have ample material; just come to Windslow Street. Indeed, Geraldine had ushered herself in at her dad's house. Her entry was full of the kind of theatrics that producers long for. Her arms were flailing about, and her large, violet eyes resembled those of a child's china doll, astonished and unblinking. Geraldine babbled on and on, loud and raucous, with a mixture of vulgarity and multi-syllable words, speaking a kind of glossolalia. One would think that a lady would not speak like that, especially this one. Most of what she said was confused gibberish, and neither Joliana nor her father could figure it. It was like Geraldine had crashed to earth from another planet. She made absolutely no sense. Yet she and her father had persisted in this game of charades until it became an unsettling shouting match. Something had jettisoned Geraldine from her nest; something had prompted Geraldine to override her fears and complacency. What had this woman seen or experienced? Joliana certainly wanted to understand so she could help this woman. Her stomach did a somersault. Awful indigestion. She wanted to figure what was happening with her dad and with Lizzie and, heavens, with herself! She had not even made that call to the police station! Life had become a giant obstacle course, and she was trailing badly. Oh, Lord what should she do? And what about that letter? What other scary goblin would be staring at her? She needed to plan. Once she settled Geraldine in, she would decide what to do next.

Joe watched his daughter walk Geraldine home. She was always running off, although this time it was for the best. Joliana was very smart. She had figured that his bruised head was no accident. He had not fallen at all; that damn Pete had roughed him up. He surveyed his living quarters. The laid back look had taken on an unsettled appearance. Pete had styled his home into the trashed look. Books, newspapers, condiments, and muddy shoes were strewn everywhere. Pete had truly taken on the persona of a hungry grizzly who was sniffing out lunch. And Pete had become more agitated by the moment, breaking all kinds of stuff in his path. Joe smirked. Pete had found a portion of the gold nugget he had been seeking: the Smith & Wesson, that sweet hand gun. Oh well. A scary scowl then turned into a mischievous smile. Pete had commandeered the aged weapon, but he didn't have the pot of gold, not at all. Hank had most of that, perhaps buried on some tropical island or maybe, just maybe, in his own backyard. But he had his compensation—not the big bucks, but he had gotten a good slice. So damn them all! They had called him a coward; they had pronounced him yellow, but he had had life decisions to make. Joe pursed his lips. Back then, he had a wife and kids to consider. He certainly didn't want them in harm's way. So he had bailed from that frenetic rollercoaster ride. Pete and Hank had called him a traitor, but he had done the right thing as a father. These accusations made his blood boil! Joe grabbed the worn straw broom and harshly pushed some of the broken crockery aside. Joe looked down on the patterned shards that seemed to sum up his life. Broken. Discarded. Abandoned. His wife was dead; his daughters were not there for him. Gosh, Joliana was no help, and she was just across the street. And God only knows where the other one had ended up. He was a dejected, sour old man. Joe hung his head in disgust. He then kicked the pile of strewn newspapers. "How dare they!" he said aloud. Damn, he was doing it again, vacillating between molten anger and depression like a menopausal woman. Joe stood in the middle of the kitchen, holding the broom handle straight and secure. It was right here. He hadn't looked in some time, but he could tell by the nick in the yellowed green and brown linoleum. Joe chuckled aloud. *Pete will never find this secret place, ever!* The broom dropped to the floor as Joe knelt close to the cracked tile. He fiddled in his pants pocket and found his trusted army knife. With the blunt edge of the implement, Joe gingerly eased up the flooring, revealing a compartment underneath. It was a secret hiding space he had rigged himself, and he was proud of it. He stuck his hand in the underlying floorboards, fingering for a metal container. It was lodged in place, snug through all the years of kitchen rambling, hidden from the ordinary culinary events of making creamed beef and toasted cheese sandwiches.

This was his little stash, all his. Joe patted the cold metal. It had been given to him as hush money so that the bank manager would not be implicated. Joe smiled. This same executive was thrust into the limelight only to lose his life shortly after in a horrific car crash, a crash he was certain was not an accident. Joe had been paid off in the nick of time, a grand total of seventy-five thousand dollars. Not bad, not bad at all. Should he take it out and count it again to make sure it was all there? Maybe even take a portion of it and spend it since he had been so frugal? Joe felt an icy tingle stroke his spine and he shuddered. Not now, not with Pete around. Joe abruptly dropped the flooring in place and stepped hard on it. No, it wasn't yet time for this greenback to see the light of day.

Chapter Nineteen

Burt's Lunch. As usual, the place was hopping, so Jerry parked haphazardly in a direction opposite to the other vehicles. On a good day, he would present citations to residents who had done this very thing. After all, he wasn't just living in this stupid town; he was a home-grown police officer. He figured the town owed him after twenty-plus years of service. And those years in high school, well, he would never forget the awful things the kids did to him. It was as close to a college fraternity hazing as they come. He remembered one time he was pressured to steal canned goods from the dining hall. He did pretty well at first; he efficiently disconnected the alarm system and busted the lock. Then he piled the goods into a box and attempted to leave, when he met with the school patrolman, a husky, no-nonsense kind of guy. At the time, he had no idea where he had gone wrong, until he eavesdropped and heard one of his so-called buddy's malign him. Indeed, it was the very gang that he had tried so hard to accommodate that turned on him that night and called the authorities. He would never forget the taunting. Now it was payback time. His life as a police officer had allowed him to barely skirt the way of justice, providing ample opportunity for many backroom dealings. He had found his revenge and had never been caught. He was definitely one step ahead of everyone else and intended to keep it that way.

Jerry pulled the stretched elastic band tighter on his salt-and-pepper ponytail and headed into the fifties-style diner. He could almost swear that he just walked into a black and white photograph, resplendent with its old-fashioned mahogany and marble, with blaring signs of popular refreshments from the past. The savory scents of beef and onions catapulted him back. Jerry licked the side of his mouth as his saliva thickened and threatened to ooze down his chin. He nodded a brief greeting to the other lunching officers and settled into his usual small booth in a dimly lit corner.

"Well, what will it be today?" said the older waitress with eyes that boasted two pounds of blue and black Maybelline glamour.

Damn, he had gotten this lady again. Why couldn't one of those blond chicks wait on him? He felt irritated but his keen hunger overruled. "I want a couple of your hamburger specials, with extra cheese and onions and a heap of fries." He had not eaten all day and he could be nasty when he got hungry.

"Anything to drink?"

"Hot, hot coffee, your strongest brew, and make sure that it's fresh."

"Will that be all?"

Jerry nodded and looked away.

"Jerry … it is Jerry, isn't it?"

Jerry nodded again.

"Why is it you always sit by yourself, and your friends sit way over there?" said the woman. As she pointed her arm, the ample fat and flab wiggled and jiggled.

Jerry grunted. He caught the woman's eyes and gave those blackened peepers one of his meanest glares. As far as he was concerned, he owed this lady nothing.

The waitress persisted. "It's just that you're such a loner, and you seem to do things much differently than your friends."

"What kind of things do I do different?" Now Jerry was both agitated and curious. What on earth was this woman talking about? Yes, he liked to work alone; he really didn't care that others on the force would avoid him. Yes, he did things his own way, but that was not this woman's concern.

"It's just that over the years, you seem to be at the oddest places at the strangest times. Every time I pick up the newspaper, I wonder."

"Like what places, for instance?" said Jerry, his anger mounting.

"Well, for example, you were at the robbery at that dairy store … I believe it's called Marty's Complete. And then shortly after, you were seen at the Staller place. Seems funny, that's all."

"What's funny about that? I'm just doing my job, that's all. Besides, it's none of your business where I go."

"To the contrary, I'm a paying citizen and I have the right to know what is going on in my town, and I know a lot of people feel the same way."

Jerry's snarled, his upper lip menacingly curled. "Woman, again, what's it to you and these others who have snouts way too big for their faces?"

"I hear lots of stuff, like the big bank hit twenty years ago … there's been talk for years that you were involved and that you got a good cut of …"

"Shut up, you ridiculous woman! You stupid, ugly cow! You know nothing, absolutely nothing!"

The waitress glared at Jerry, her eyes opened and unblinking.

Jerry stared back.

The woman's large neck muscles thickened and twisted.

Jerry's shoulders arched; his biceps inflated with each incensed thought. The arm then lifted off the table.

The waitress threw her full figure to one side, just missing contact with Jerry's strong fist. There was a momentary standoff like the climax found in the old western movies.

"Don't you touch me!" said the outraged woman.

The diner became silent as a morgue. All heads were cocked in their direction.

"Woman, I wouldn't come near you if you begged me!" Jerry abruptly pushed himself away from the table, his western-style boots pounding the worn hardwood floor as he left the greasy bacon-and-smoke-filled diner.

Reaching into his deep coat pocket, he dipped into his stash of flavored jelly beans and threw a handful into his mouth. This would have to do for the time being.

Chapter Twenty

Joliana efficiently settled Geraldine into the lovely caned rocker and carefully tucked a rainbow-colored afghan around her. It was probably crafted by Geraldine herself. The older woman nodded gratefully and then a thin smile crossed her face. "Could you please make me a cup of tea?" she asked with childlike hopefulness.

Joliana leaned forward towards her neighbor, awed that, finally, she had really spoken. "Of course. Just direct me to the kitchen."

Geraldine lifted her blanketed arm and waved toward the back of the house. Joliana made her way to the quaint kitchen, which was full of lacy doilies and hanging ferns. The built-in corner hutches were especially nice, and they boasted all kind of crystal and blue willow patterns.

"Oh dear, you'll find the tea in the canister over the sink and the honey in the pantry. The tea cups are in the far cupboard."

Joliana chuckled. Geraldine was finally talking. It wasn't much, but it was something. Now to make the tea and then she would find the phone and get down to business. She moved swiftly about the kitchen as if familiar with her surroundings, which she was not; it was just that Geraldine has used common sense in her organization. It had been many years since she had visited this house. Joliana was perhaps in her early teens at the time. However, she was not too young to note that some people seem to loathe others and that both Geraldine and Lizzie were untouchables. "Stay away from those crazies," was the reaction of the neighborhood. So Joliana had been swept into all the gossip, but now she was determined to figure this out. The kettle soon began sizzling and chirping. Time for tea.

Then the phone rang.

Geraldine sprang from her perch and picked up the receiver. She paused. A look of disappointment flashed across her face. "It's for you."

"For me?" Joliana quickly placed the tea-laden tray before the older woman. "Hello," she said a bit hesitantly.

"Joliana, this is Dad calling. Tony just called wondering if you were here. He says it's urgent. I told him that you were at Geraldine's. He's coming to get you in a few minutes."

"What is going on? Why the urgency? Are the kids okay? Is he all right?"

"He didn't say. Just be ready. You might want to watch out the window or go outside."

"Joliana, dear, please come sit here with me. I have to tell you about …"

"Wait a minute, Dad." Joliana then cupped the phone with her slender hand. "Geraldine, I would love to stay and have a cozy chat over tea, but my husband is coming to get me."

"Mrs. Faracelli, I have to tell you something very important," said Geraldine in a persistent tone.

"Dad, I have to go. I'll call you soon. Please continue to put ice on your forehead."

The resonant tones of a truck horn began.

"Geraldine, I have to go."

"Joliana, please wait, dear. Let me tell you about Lizzie. Something's going to happen to her, something very bad."

"What about Lizzie?" said Joliana impatiently. She tried so hard to get this woman to talk and she chooses to speak now, when she had to leave.

"I saw her, I saw her," began Geraldine, her hand trembling, the herbal concoction sloshing from side to side in the dainty cup.

"What did you see?"

"I saw Lizzie get shoved by this strange man, and then he carried her down the hatchway to the basement."

"Where did you see this happen?" Joliana felt the roots of her hair tingle. Just a short while ago, she had witnessed the same thing, but she hadn't noticed Geraldine.

"I'm not sure. Someplace with a lot of trees. I can see it in my mind. You must think I'm crazy but I did see him."

"In your mind? Geraldine, what exactly are you saying? Did you see Lizzie and that strange man?"

"I mean that it all hasn't happened yet, but it will, it will," said Geraldine with a most authoritative voice. "But you don't believe me, do you?"

Joliana grasped Geraldine's arm with a comforting touch. "It's just that I really think you saw something and it wasn't just in your mind."

The truck horn was now blaring as if Tony had jammed it in place.

Joliana lifted the delicate curtain and squinted from the late afternoon sun. "Sorry, I have to leave now. As soon as I can, I will come back, and then you can tell me everything. In the meantime, try to stay warm, and perhaps you can keep away from that perch in the attic."

Geraldine nodded weakly. Joliana sighed as she rushed out the door. She knew that Geraldine wasn't about to listen to her, but maybe it was for the best. They could certainly use a beacon in this neighborhood. She just hoped that Geraldine would stay safe in her warm, welcoming home.

Tony's large hands gripped the thick steering wheel in his new wide-angled truck. His veins seem to pulsate through his ample muscles. Joliana almost didn't want to see his face. She hopped into the high-set passenger's seat and positioned her head towards the tinted window, pretending to be enthralled by the gray and white landscape.

"So what is going on with you, Joliana?"

"With me? You called me with this urgency. You tell me."

"Something's strange, that's all I can tell you." Tony muttered a couple of angry Italian phrases that he threw out whenever he was upset.

"Well, try me. I've had a full day of peculiar stuff. In fact, the past two days have been such a whirlwind that I'm not sure what's going on."

"It has to do with Marty's Mart."

"What's going on now?"

"Yeah, it's a funny thing, but Steve and Mary said that they saw you when it happened."

"Saw me? When what happened?"

"When the robbery happened. They saw you, said you were one of the thieves. You had another woman with you. She had long hair and was wearing lots of dark clothing." Tony cocked his head menacingly towards his wife. "So, Joliana, what is going on?"

Joliana felt as if she were pinned to her bed during a traumatic dream. Outside her window, trees, farmhouses, and rolling hills passed by. Normal stuff. Yet she was stuck in some kind of miry bog that was getting worse. She looked over at her irate husband, who was now hollering in ear-deadening staccato tones. How dare he talk to her like this!

"What are you saying, Tony? Are you accusing me of raiding that store—mind you, one of our own stores—and lying about it? Is that what you're saying?"

"Listen, woman, I'm not suggesting anything. I'm telling you. What's the matter with you? Are you so unhappy with your life that you would get involved in such a mess?"

Joliana's mouth went dry. How could he say these things? Here she was, his faithful, diligent wife for all these years, and he attacks her like this? "That woman wasn't me. I told you the whole story *just this morning. You believed me then.*" Joliana sat upright and glared at her husband.

"Yeah, right."

"When I tell you I didn't do something, I mean it!" She wasn't a welcome doormat any longer.

"Well, that same woman that you claim is not you was also wearing a bracelet very much like the one I gave you; you know, the one I found for your birthday last year?"

"Bracelet?" Joliana squirmed in her seat. She hadn't realized that her special piece was missing. It was a wonderful piece of jewelry, with unique charms that her husband and kids had specially purchased, but at times the clanging on her wrist became very annoying and she would take it off.

"Well, where did the police find it?"

"The police said they noted it on the surveillance tape." Tony cast that hurt puppy look at her, his large blue eyes sad and questioning. Joliana shrugged and turned away. How she hated that look.

Tony slowed the truck and leaned his head. "I'm all ears."

"Remember last night evening when I went out and came back really late?"

"Yeah, we talked about it this morning, and I thought that you had leveled with me."

"Let me tell you again. When I realized that I had lost my cards, I decided to pay Marty's Complete a late visit. When I got there, I found yellow police tape securing the front of the store, which I should have expected with the robbery and all. I took out my key to get in, but found that the door was ajar, and I saw a light moving about. It was like a cigarette or a small flashlight."

"Then what did you do?"

"The dark store and the light unnerved me. It just didn't feel right. So I got out of there. That is probably when the bracelet fell off."

"Let me see if I have this right. You went alone to Marty's quite late to look again for your cards. Something scared you, and that's when you left. But the bracelet I don't get. If it fell off your wrist last night, then how come the robber was seen wearing it?"

Joliana's could feel her cheeks redden. Why had she said that? She had probably left it on the rear room desk. How could she be so stupid? Somehow, one of the burglars had made off with her piece. But now this was all sounding like a far fetched fairy tale.

"So?" Tony eyed his wife with curiosity.

"I'm, not sure how that happened. But there's something else. When I pulled out of the lot, a police cruiser came in. I felt really nervous, so I floored the gas. I was sure he was following me, but when I looked back, he wasn't."

"Joliana, why did you leave in the first place? After all, you had the right to be there. You could have checked things out, maybe even talked to the cop."

"It didn't feel right."

"Joliana, you should have talked to the police! That was stupid!"

"But, Tony, I wasn't supposed to be there!"

"And why not? We're part owners of that store. You had every right to stay! By running, you made yourself look guilty!" Tony pointed his finger angrily at Joliana. "Maybe that's because you are!"

"That's not so! Haven't you heard a word I've said? I'm your wife. Whose side are you on, anyhow?"

Tony grabbed onto Joliana's wrist. "I'm sick of the lies and the games. I want you to level with me now before we go to Marty's store and talk to the police!"

"Let me out right now," shouted Joliana as she pulled away from her husband's grasp and pushed on the door handle. "I'll jump if you don't stop!"

Tony ranted at his wife but slowly let his foot let up on the pedal.

Joliana did not waste time. In a moment, she had slid from the truck and begun her jog down the street.

Chapter Twenty-One

Geraldine paced in front of the lace-adorned picture window, forlornly watching Joliana hop into her husband's truck. She had tried to tell Joliana about Lizzie, but the sense of urgency in her story was lacking. She believed Joliana had not taken her seriously. Lizzie still needed help, and as much as Lizzie was as flaky as they come, Geraldine considered her a friend. In fact, she was perhaps her only friend. Once upon a time, Geraldine had been connected; she had had a life. She walked over to the stuffed bookshelf and pulled out a photo album. Its binding was cracked and shredded, and the cover mildewed. As she threw it open, dust and the dank smell of old ink filled her nostrils, causing her to sputter and wheeze. Most of the black and white photos were proudly displayed four to a page, with a Payne's gray anchor at each corner. They had been arranged with great artistry, although as she thumbed through, some photos hung precariously and others fell around her feet.

Geraldine smiled to herself. Just the other day, she had perused another album she had found in the attic loft, and here she was, at it again. Ah! There she was, standing next to Lizzie at some sort of picnic. Lizzie was dressed appropriately for the occasion in her clam digger pants and frilly blouse, although she had chosen an odd mixture of stripes and plaids that resembled wallpaper prints. The smudged smirk was there, and even though it was only represented in gray tones, Geraldine could see the candied apple coloration in her mind's eye. And yes, the huge black sunglasses cast a shadow across Lizzie's face, creating a certain mystique.

Geraldine held the picture closer to her bifocals. Where were they? She scanned the photo, taking in all the minute details of the room. Indeed, they were at Joe Williard's home; she could see a teenage Joliana in the background and Joe's wife off to the left. Indeed, Mrs. Williard was very busy ironing. Yes, ironing something that fell over the side of the ironing board. It was strangely familiar. Where had she seen it? Then she remembered. In the other photo book, she had seen this material fashioned like a cape around the neck of one of Mr. Williard's friends. She placed the photo closer to her nose. Some robust man was bent down, fingering the material on the ironing board. Geraldine gasped. She recognized who it was … it was Hank Staller! Mr. Williard and Hank were in the same house, the arch rivals actually rubbing elbows. And there was another man. Ah, wait a minute! Geraldine's hand began to shake and her throat went dry. She knew this man; she had just seen him— with Lizzie. Geraldine's throaty wail vibrated off the wall of the tranquil living room. Thick cobwebs fell from her brain. It was a man named Peter Smaltz. Yes, the three had been feuding for many years, but some activity had brought them together, and the warring stopped briefly only to become fiercer than ever.

In the dim background, one other figure remained. Geraldine had to squeeze her eyes nearly shut to make the person out. The fact that the photo had discolored, causing the figure to blend into sienna tones, didn't help. The gastric juices rose from deep in her stomach and coated her lips. The other person was James, her dearly betrothed. Why in the world was he there? Why was he mingling with these strange men? Geraldine was incredulous, her mouth open wide and her hand quivering. Actually, the question was why was she there? After all, she had taken the picture! She remembered taking the photo but had no recollection of why they were at the Williard home. Then she remembered something, a very sad event from back then. It was about this time that her dear fiancé had had an accident on Route 29. It had been frigid weather, like it was now, and he had hit an ice patch. Her dear, dear James never made it to the hospital. Geraldine's eyes reddened, and a single eye drop streaked down her cheek. She would never forget that she lost her love, her profession, her life. The trauma had sucked away her very lifeblood. She became a changed person, one who, instead of choosing to conquer the world, had not been able to even leave her own house.

The rumble of a large vehicle startled Geraldine. She ambled up the staircase to the top of the loft. Darn, she had missed the truck. She was just darn slow these days. But what was this? Geraldine swooped up a yellowed newsprint article that must have dropped out the other day. She began to read, mumbling some words aloud. It highlighted the details of the huge heist that had happened in the town's largest bank some twenty years ago. Her gaze froze on three sentences: "Only one of the two men was apprehended, and that was due to his failure to remove his entire costume. Some of the Superman cape had torn and was hanging off his rear pocket. Much to his chagrin, he was unable to fly away from the law."

Who was this man, anyway? Geraldine took off her bifocals and adjusted them to get a better view of the grainy picture. It was the same strange man she had seen in the photo downstairs! Her brain swirled with several possible scenarios. She became dizzy, and she could almost hear the rapid beating of her heart. My God! The whole lot of them, Hank, Joe, and that other man Pete, were in cahoots, robbing the same bank she had worked at for years and of which her fiancé had been assistant manager. And that awful man had Lizzie! Her neck twitched and her large hands quivered. Her friend was in trouble, big trouble!

Geraldine rushed down from the attic, threw on her camel hair coat, and twisted a green plaid scarf around her chilled neck. Before she could think another thought, she was out the door, for the second time.

Joliana hedged about the ice patches and muddy chunks of snow. She had better slow her pace or end up with some part of her anatomy broken. This crazy wintry obstacle course was like the past few days of her life: a dangerous downhill slope. As she slipped and sloshed her way through her keen agitation, she found her temperature rising. How dare Tony talk to her like that? How could he say such stupid things! She knew him to be a hot head and, at times, extremely opinionated, but this time his accusations were battering and unnerving. Why, Tony was her best friend. She had confided everything to him all these years, at least most everything. While he didn't share in her faith and a multitude of Christian activities, he had been supportive and encouraging to her. There must be some kind of misunderstanding here. Maybe she had heard him wrong. Maybe she had just been too sensitive and defensive. Joliana slowed her pace and recounted the conversation. Yes, she had been right; he had accused her of stealing, robbing their own store! How could he even consider she would do such a thing? But he did seem to believe what the workers saw that day, that she was one of the thieves. She was stumped by this. Perhaps they had seen someone who reminded them of her. It could be that she was all wrong in judging Tony; maybe he knew something that she didn't. It could be that she just didn't have all the pieces. Joliana began to overheat. The rapid pace, the heavy layering of clothing, and intense emotions were suffocating her. She stopped and grabbed onto a broken picket fence. Taking in several gulps of icy air, she collected herself.

These last couple of days were like a tumble weed that had rolled every twig, dust mite, and hair ball into itself. Her peace-loving manner and even pacing was out of control. The world seemed to have severely tilted off its axis, and she was barely holding on. Marty's Mart had been robbed and her license and credit card were missing. She believed her dad had been assaulted, and Geraldine was seriously agitated by something that happened to Lizzie. Topping all of this off, her husband was accusing her of theft. Oh, then there was that strange birth certificate that evidenced she didn't even know who she was! What else could go wrong? Somehow, all this should make some kind of sense; there was a connection between things that she just wasn't seeing. Yes, that could be it. If she could just figure out key pieces of this puzzle, maybe things would fall into place. What she needed was clarity, not the murky New England waters of the Sound. Prayer often helped, but she hadn't spent any time asking for God's opinion. This would have to change, and she promised herself that she would take a few moments soon.

Joliana looked around. Windslow Street. Finally. She was getting pretty sick of tracking down this road, but all she had to do was travel the mile or so to her house. The wintry day was waning, the sky lovely with a splash of vermillion and crimson rose. On the periphery were several ominous clouds that were clotting together, attempting to diminish the glory of the setting sun. It was an awesome sight, but Joliana was paying little attention. She just had to get past all these houses with their hodgepodge assortment of strange folks. Crazy Lizzie over there in that rundown bungalow, and next door was Mr. Tymes, the man who collected everything, and the excess items served as front lawn decorations. Joliana chuckled aloud. Most of those items were buried under snow drifts, showing only bit and pieces, resembling some sort of pop art. There was Miss Saunders, the resident bookworm, who wrote endless essays although she had never published one, and Mrs. Boers, the divorced ballet dancer, who one day stuck her leg in a pail of dry ice so that the tissue and the leg under the knee had to be amputated. The woman had some issues, and Joliana would have loved to have talked with her, but this neighbor never opened her door. Then there was the Gruder family, who were all too gregarious for her, having wild parties all the time; often, the grand finale would be a visit from the local police. Of course, on the other side of the street was Geraldine's house. She was a recluse of many years, who had chosen this afternoon to go out. Joliana's sigh seemed to crystallize in the frigid air. She was surrounded by all these odd people and she was beginning to feel like them, confused and crazy. But right now, she was really cold. She stared down at her drenched boots, numb and wet with the cold. Her legs felt rubbery from so much walking, and her stomach was making sounds that one would only hear out in the woods. Joliana rubbed her chilled cheeks. Soon she would be in her warm kitchen, sipping some hot chocolate and reading that strange letter. She would be home any minute.

What was that? It was a thin wail of sorts. It could be a dog or maybe a person, and it seemed to come from across the street at Hank's place. She felt extremely conflicted; part of her wished to run home as fast as she could, as if wearing blinders, and the other part, the curious sleuth side, wanted to stay and explore. Joliana began crossing the street. She just couldn't help herself. She had to find out what was going on. Joliana approached with a loud, determined step. In the distance, she saw a flash of tan and white. She stepped closer, following the line of cedar trees to the backyard. Was something moving? Joliana edged closer even though a good part of her wanted to scurry to the safety of one of those protective evergreens. A green cloth of sorts was caught in a branch and waving in the frigid wind. Joliana grabbed the rippling material and surveyed the plaid scarf she now held in her hands. It appeared familiar. Thump. Joliana fell forward but quickly righted herself. Darn, she must have lost her footing on a branch or tree stump. She planted her boots into the snow and turned to check out the obstacle. Joliana's mouth hung open but no sound was forthcoming. It was Geraldine—and she wasn't moving.

Chapter Twenty-Two

Marty's Complete was anything but a peaceful rest stop. Two police vehicles had planted themselves flush to the entrance. Yellow caution tape was swirled about haphazardly, like modern art. Tony's beefy cheeks remained flushed as he answered question after question. A visit from the police was worse than a surprise visit from your friendly neighborhood tax auditor. They had figured him to be the guilty party, at the very least aiding and abetting Joliana. They focused on awful accusations involving embezzlement and bankruptcy. Many questions were derived from the incriminating tape, and they were playing it over and over. Initially, he was so confounded that he was ready to throw up his hands in surrender. But now Tony was not so sure. Although the thieves had attempted to destroy the tape, its grainy contents adequately profiled the robbery. However, the angles were all wrong. While this blond lady resembled his wife, she was not Joliana. She was a definite look alike, but she was not his wife. He had never seen Joliana in that coat, and her stance was all wrong. And who was that other woman with her, the one with the dark hair that was pulled back and secured under a baseball cap? Certainly he knew his wife's friends; her people were his people. Heck, he knew Joliana, and this woman was not someone he recognized.

"Wait, please back up the tape a bit," asked Tony.

The policeman smirked and rewound the tape.

"There! I can't put my finger in it, but I'm sure that this woman is not my wife." Tony stared hard at the tape, his hand stroking his cheek.

"Yeah, well, we're waiting. Can't stay here all day."

"Just give me a minute ..."

"The way it looks, Mr. Faracelli, is that we have a pretty good suspect here, and what we need is your cooperation to bring in your wife in for questioning."

"Wait, I see it! Right here. Both women have taken off their party masks and one of them is saying something to her friend. Just look at her mouth!"

The police officer with the full midriff leaned closer to the tape. "I don't see what you're seeing. Besides, the tape isn't that clear," he said in an irritated voice.

"Yeah, I don't know either. Looks like you're stalling for time," said Officer Jerry as he adjusted his long, gray ponytail.

"Right here. This woman has the worst set of teeth I have ever seen. If you were to meet Joliana, you would know the difference. My wife has never missed a dental appointment her entire life, and when she smiles, she could easily be chosen for a toothpaste commercial. The real suspect is somewhere out there," said Tony, adamantly pointing his finger towards the door.

The balding officer bent his lumbering girth and watched the footage more carefully. Jerry played with the leather of his gun strap and walked back and forth, like an impatient father to be. He was in no mood for this.

"Mr. Faracelli, we just need to find your wife. Now, if you could cooperate," said Jerry in rough tones.

"You know, Jerry, maybe Mr. Faracelli is on to something here. This young woman has some dental problems," said the overweight officer.

"Yeah, yeah, and she's wearing two left socks and her coat is on backwards." Jerry began tapping his leather boot on the side of the chair. "But she is wearing a bracelet that your wife has often been seen wearing. Just how do you explain that?"

Tony ignored Jerry's remark. "Didn't you hear me? I believe we have to look for someone else. You guys need to get to work fingerprinting, dusting, or whatever it is that you do to find clues!" Tony murmured some additional angry remarks that were peppered with his native Italian tongue.

"It's been done. Evidence has been taken. However, since this is not a murder or physical assault crime scene, certain items, such as a murder weapon, are not available. But speaking of fingerprints, we have lots of them; we might even have the entire town in this evidence bag."

Tony shrugged. The officer was right, of course. Everyone's hands were touching this and that. It was a good thing one couldn't see all the smudges, especially his wife; it would make her go wild! Joliana liked her antiseptic, Mr. Clean world. "Please, officers, just give me a few more moments with this tape."

"You've got five minutes and that's it! I've got to wrap this up and get back to the station," said the robust policeman, who was beginning to lose his composure. Then he ambled down the pastry aisle, checking out the coffee cakes.

Jerry's bushy left eyebrow arched, resembling the virgin territory of the early West, which had clearly never seen either scythe or tweezers. His lips spread from ear to ear in a wide smile. Yes, this was getting interesting.

Tony again reviewed the final portion of the film where both women had removed their facial guises, probably figuring they had already done their business in wrecking cameras and tying up the night staff. He stared hard at the lady who was supposed be his wife. He squinted closely at her hand. It wasn't there; the lovely tear-shaped diamond was missing. "Come over and see this!"

Both policemen sauntered over. "Okay, what is it now?" asked Jerry.

"Right here, don't you see it? There, on her left hand, there is not a stitch of jewelry. Why, my wife wears a lovely wedding band and engagement ring fashioned in the finest gold and diamonds, as well as a customized mother's ring with the birthstones of our three children. You see, there's nothing there."

Jerry shrugged. The other officer looked on indifferently, licking the remainder of lemon icing off his fingers.

"We'll have to see about that," said Jerry.

"Yeah, I guess so, but for now, we're done here," said his partner.

"But, but we haven't finished here yet. We have other possibilities," stammered Tony.

"We're done for now," said Jerry as he opened the front door for Tony with one hand and slipped a handful of jelly beans in his mouth with the other.

Tony's snow- and dirt-encrusted work boots were positioned as if velcroed to the gas and clutch pedals. He was so incensed that he could have really smacked those cops at the store. But while a wrestling match would have felt great, time in the slammer was not to his liking. So he would drive like he was in a Nascar competition, like the renowned Jeff Gordon. Tony twisted and turned down the back roads of the small town. The winding blacktop was sun-drenched in spots and snow-caked and slippery in others. Yet his hands drove on automatic while his mind dashed about in a rapid sequence of scenes, creating a descriptive montage. He couldn't believe the gall those officers had to harass him and rudely accuse his wife of armed burglary. They put down his Joliana! She stood falsely accused. But just a short while before, he had also pointed a jagged finger at his wife. What had he been thinking? Tony pumped the gas pedal a little harder. Despite the frigid temperature, his hands were warm and clammy, and his ears were bright crimson, evidence of his inner rage. But right now, his stomach held a hollow ache, like a pumpkin that had been cleaned out. He knew this feeling; this wasn't just anger, but guilt with a huge side order of shame.

Tony squirmed in his seat, pulling at his full moustache, which adorned his mouth, allowing only a slight hint of his bottom lip. His naturally reddened complexion was aflame, and his electric blue eyes were angled downward as if ready to squeeze out a tear or two. But Tony didn't cry, never had as far as he could remember. Maybe once in third grade he almost did when Tom, the class bully, who they had called Tom the Ton, came after him. This boy was scary to behold, his face all pocked and filled with blackheads and his belly wiggling full of chocolate cakes. Yeah, he was scared and he had almost started bawling; he almost jumped the broken-down, rusty fence. But Tony didn't. Instead, he rolled back his sleeve and swung his arm around in a complete circle, his fist squarely meeting the bully's nose. He had put that kid in his place, and now it was time to put the cops in their place. They weren't going to treat his wife like that. He would head back and look for Joliana. The wintry afternoon sun dipped way down in the sky as Tony turned his truck toward home.

Chapter Twenty-Three

Joliana recoiled. This shouldn't be happening, but it was. Geraldine, the neighbor down the street, with whom she had just had tea, was lying helpless, face down, on the ground. Well, actually, her head was tilted a bit to the right so that she wasn't swallowing snow. The elderly lady lay still, too still. Joliana straightened her scarf and rewound it about her neck, uncertain what to do. The next instant, she jumped into action, checking Geraldine's vitals. Joliana's nursing knowledge was not comprehensive, but she knew enough to at least assess her friend. She was able to note a pulse, although very weak. The woman was still breathing in a most irregular pattern. Joliana sighed. The woman's color was all wrong as well. Gone were the high-arched, naturally peach cheeks that she had seen just a short time before. Instead, a pasty grayish color stared back at her. Geraldine's eyes were clamped shut, her mouth slightly open. What had happened here? Had she been bludgeoned with some kind of heavy object or had she been shot? Maybe it was simply that she had slipped on an icy patch and fallen. Joliana had to look every bit of Geraldine over like some kind of private detective, except she had to be careful not to move her; what if her neck had been broken? Just the thought of it made the hairs on the nape of her neck stand straight. Beginning with the older woman's head, Joliana knelt down and gently touched the scalp, ear, neck, and shoulder. Nothing seemed out of the ordinary. There was no sign of blood or any evidence of an entrance or exit wound. Joliana eased two of the root beer barrel buttons open, exposing the layering of sweaters and lace beneath, which was no easy task since Geraldine was laying on most of her bunched coat. Then she scanned the thick nylon stocking leg wear, probably the kind that was used to improve circulation, but came up with little more than huge runs and minor cuts. Nothing, absolutely nothing. She must have missed something. Joliana muttered aloud, "Help me, God!" which was the closest to praying she had done these last two days. Gosh, did she ever need assistance, and some divine intervention would come in handy right about now. She had a sense to look again at the back of Geraldine's head, this time taking in a right-sided view. Using her long, slender fingers, Joliana gently worked her way through the silver hair, some of which had fallen from the tightly fashioned bun. Then she stopped. There was a definite bump on the back of the skull, and as she pulled back her hand, she noted a wet, slick feeling. Blood. Joliana again surveyed the area. Geraldine could have tripped over these twigs or the thick brush. She stooped to the snow-covered ground. There were lots of footprints, or rather boot prints, and she could identify her own and Geraldine's. But who was the owner of the thick boot print that almost resembled tire treading? Could this be the unwelcome assailant? Or was she operating with too great of an imagination?

But then again, why had Geraldine been out here in the first place? Everyone knew that this woman wasn't one to leave her house ever, yet she had been out today. Twice. It was just too bad. Perhaps the elderly Peeping Tom knew something, and maybe she went out to find it. Whatever it was, right now Geraldine wasn't talking, and if she didn't find a good medic and fast, she might never speak again. Joliana unzipped her beloved blue pea coat and gently eased it over Geraldine. Then she pulled her favorite red scarf from her neck and, fashioning it like a small pillow, she slipped it under the older woman's cheek, cushioning her from the snow. Joliana was peeled down to her maroon turtleneck but she was not shivering; indeed, she felt more flushed than ever. What should she do? Just leave Geraldine on the ground? But this woman needed medical attention. Joliana had to get help. Was there anyone around? She saw movement in the brush. Could that be an assailant coming back to finish the job? Chocolate fur leaped from the snow into Joliana's arms. Boomer.

"Boomer, I'm so glad you're here, but you really startled me." The Labrador finished licking Joliana's face and then sniffed and nudged at Geraldine. "Boomer, this lady is hurt. I'm not sure what to do."

The dog walked about Geraldine's quiet form and then secured himself close to her, his loyal eyes alert and concerned.

Casting a hopeful look at Geraldine and faithful Boomer, Joliana turned and let her legs carry her like those of an Olympian athlete. She traversed Windslow Street like she used to when she was a kid in shorts wearing her broken in P. F. Flyer sneakers. In good time, Joliana dashed into her home, dirty boots casting snow and mud everywhere. The other Joliana would never have done that; instead, the boots would have been carefully removed in the adjoining mud room and cleaned off. But right now, she just didn't care. All she wanted was the telephone and, hopefully, the help it would bring.

"This is 911. Can I help you?"

"Yes, yes, my name is Joliana Faracelli. There's a problem here; a woman has been hurt."

"Tell me what is happening with this woman."

"I'm not quite sure, but she is lying down in the snow and she is not moving. There's a bump in back of her head and she's bleeding."

"Miss, can you tell me where you are?"

"Ah, I'm calling from home but the woman I saw is on the Staller property, the two-floor white bungalow with the garage that is leaning over. I believe that the address is 67 Windslow Street."

"Can you identify this woman?"

"Yes, I can. She's Ms. Geraldine Pryor, who also lives on this street."

"The paramedics are on their way. They should arrive soon, within twenty minutes or so."

"Twenty minutes? But what if …?" She was peeved. In that amount of time, Geraldine could be found dead. It was a good thing Boomer was there, keeping vigil. All the same, she was becoming less and less enamored with this cozy New England town. Meeting the paramedics was a priority, but now she did have time to call Tony at the mart and leave a note for the kids so that they wouldn't worry when they couldn't find her. Her usually nimble fingers went all spastic as she attempted to dial the numbers. Damn this old phone! Nerves. She was wound more tightly than the coveted vintage clock she kept on the mantel. Joliana plopped herself onto the high-backed Colonial couch. She just needed a moment to think, but as she sat, she felt the folded edges of the peculiar document biting into her waist. She yanked the paper from her form-fitting jeans pocket. Leaning over the oak coffee table, she placed the yellowed document down and carefully smoothed the creases. As she did so, the single sheet became two.

Joliana gasped. Her jaw hung awkwardly and the rest of her froze in the perfect mime position.

There were two birth certificates before her, and they were not copies.

Joliana's intense emerald eyes danced the foxtrot from one page to another. An apt speed-reader, she was attempting to grasp what her eyes were scanning. What she was reading had to be impossible. How could this be so? Her chest cavity felt tight as her heart pounded out of control and the back of her knees became clammy and sweaty. She felt like a plastic drop cloth had fallen on her and she was smothering; she was choking. She raised her hand to her mouth as she coughed uncontrollably. She was having another panic attack, but this time it was for good reason. She could not cajole herself with positive self-talk that everything would be okay, because it wasn't. It was beyond her comprehension, but she had just discovered that she was one of two. She had a twin sister. She reviewed the two documents several times to note a possible error but noted her birth on one of the soiled pages, and on the other, the birth of a child named Bethena Judete. Another odd name. Her mother was cited as Lenadora, but the named father was someone she had never heard of, a Mr. Charles something. His handwriting was lavishly artistic; even an interpreter would be challenged by it. Under his signature, where his name had probably been typed in, was a blackened line. Magic marker. Indeed, the document was full of such alterations, and as she held it to her nose, she could faintly detect that awful aroma. Who was this man? All her life, she had known her father to be Joe Williard, an obstinate but affable man with a huge heart; and even though he would drive her crazy with his demanding behavior, she cared for him. But these documents were stating that she had been living a lie; her mother had had twins and was remarried. Or maybe she hadn't remarried. Perhaps they had lived in a common law agreement. The man she called dad was really a stepfather of sorts, while her sister and natural father were either somewhere at large or dead. Joliana's spine tingled as if a powerful current had surged through it. Her reality was a confused tangle of wires and copper tubing.

As the key met the heavy brass lock, a familiar clicking echoed through the coat room, into the kitchen. Then came the thumping and the banging and the peals of uncontrolled laughter. Joliana could hardly believe it was that time already, but the Westminster chimes confirmed that it was five o' clock. The children were home, although a bit late due to after school activities, and it sounded like a busload of day campers had been left on her doorstep. And she had wanted to leave a note and dash off to the Staller house to meet up with the police. Geraldine was out there in the cold, and it was getting dark! She looked up again at the clock. She had about ten minutes before the police came. Quickly, she stuffed the birth notices into the yarn basket.

"Hi, Mommy, are you here? We're home," bellowed the youngest daughter, Susie.

"Hi, Mom. I had hoped you were home. I've got a few math problems I need help with," echoed Brad as he continued to tease his older sister.

"Will you guys calm down? Get your hands off my hair, Brad, right now!" Karen pushed her younger brother away but he boomeranged back.

"Can't make me stop. I'm gonna find your address book and call up all your boyfriends."

Brad ran through the hall to Karen's room.

"Don't' you dare go look at my stuff!" Karen tossed her books on the kitchen table and went after her brother.

"*Will all you please shut up, and I mean right now,*" Joliana shouted.

The house went silent as if the pause button had been pushed.

Susie's lower lip quivered as the tears filled her eyes. She hurried to the Hitchcock rocker and piled the homemade Afghans about her.

"Mom, what's the matter? Did we do something wrong?" asked Brad, his eyes wide and questioning.

"What's going on, Mom? You never yell like that. Is there something bad happening? Is Dad okay?" Karen turned towards her mother, looking for a response.

Joliana felt dizzy; her hands and legs were shaking. She had erupted and she hadn't meant to. Their bickering, she just couldn't take it. Her mind swirled like a kaleidoscope of conflicting emotions. She needed to be here with her children … she needed to be helping Geraldine.

Joliana went over to her younger daughter's side. "I'm so sorry, Susie."

"I'm sorry, Mommy, if I got you mad. I'll be good." Susie threw her pudgy, baby-soft arms tightly around Joliana's neck. "How come you go away all the time?"

Joliana hugged Susie and tucked her into the blankets. She paced the kitchen, her leather boots creating long skid marks on the linoleum.

"Yeah, Mom, yesterday you went out a lot and you were not acting right," said Karen.

"Mom, what was up with that? Grandpa called all mad about everything since he said that you would have dinner. And when we looked for you, we found you had left," said Brad.

"And then I heard Daddy talking in that way he does when he gets upset. You know, he kind of yells at the wall and slams the kitchen cabinets. It took me a long time to fall asleep because Daddy was so noisy. Mommy, are you mad at Daddy? Are you going to leave us?" said Susie.

Joliana sighed. Five-year-old Susie was sucking her thumb, which she did when upset. Joliana could sense her facial muscles tightening, and her lips were pursed together, her stress signature. Heavens, there were so many questions. What should she say to them, that she had irresponsibly lost her charge card and license, and that she was wanted for a theft in her own store? And there was Lizzie's abduction and Geraldine's accident; would she be blamed for some of this, as well? To add the red cherry to this messy sundae was the fact that she was a twin to a sister she had never met, a daughter to a man she had never heard of. All this turmoil was circling her like a Midwestern twister, and her very best friend in life, Tony, was not any help at all. Instead of being an advocate, he had become her adversary like the green goblin in a kid's movie. So what part of all this could she share with her children? She believed that she had to say something. The two older ones, already in their teenage years, could handle much more than five-year-old Susie. Yet this sweet child expressed the most concern, even considering that she and Tony were ready for divorce court. Such raw insecurities. Joliana knew she had to tell them; she just had to use some wisdom. Gosh, she wished she had time to settle in her room for some time to think and pray before she had to answer. But Geraldine was still out there. She would have to go soon.

"Mommy, are you listening? You look like you've gone away, and I'm sitting right here."

"Susie, I heard you. Brad and Karen, as well. There's been a lot going on, and I need your help. Yesterday, I did a really dumb thing and lost very important cards at Marty's store: my driver's license and a major credit card. They fell out somehow. I've looked everywhere but I can't seem …"

"You did what, Mom?" started Karen. "Lost important cards like that? That's not like you at all. What were you thinking?"

Brad watched his mother, his lashes fluttering nervously. "But, Mom, why would you need a credit card at one of our own stores? Gosh, sometimes Dad just tells me to take anything I want."

"Good thinking, Brad. You're very right; I didn't need the cards. I had been working at Marty's and left all the important papers and my cards on the desk in the back office. Somehow, I forgot them. Then later on that day, the robbers came in and took them."

"So, Mom," began Susie, "you're saying that the cards were mixed up with the other work papers. This doesn't sound right, Mommy, because you are the most tidy Mommy there is. You always have everything in its place, and you're forever telling us to put our toys away."

"Yeah, Susie is right. It doesn't sound like you to just have cards loose like that. Why, the last time I went shopping, you spent so long putting them back in your wallet," said Karen.

"And," added Brad, "you have a special order for everything, especially your pocketbook. How come you were so careless? Were you sick?"

Furrows gathered, like fancy pleats in a Victorian window dressing, right down the middle of Joliana's forehead. Her usually bright, jade eyes were dimmed by the dark craters that underlined them. She sifted her hands through the sides of her corn-colored hair, patting the silky strands back. She was deep into her thinking mode. Brad and Karen, familiar with Mom's quirks, waited, but Susie squirmed impatiently. "You're all very right. Something else was going on." Joliana paused. "I believe I was distracted. There was an interesting situation occurring behind me."

"What was it, Mom? Was it a bad man, a wanted criminal like we saw on the news?" asked Brad.

"No, no, I don't think it was a man, but there were two women behind me and they were arguing. I turned my head just a bit and saw one of them. Somehow, she looked familiar to me. I remember getting flustered, and all I wanted to do was to get finished so I could come home." Joliana looked out the window. It was getting darker. Just great. Now she was remembering some important details but she would have to leave soon and check on Geraldine.

The blaring sounds of an approaching ambulance entered Windslow Street.

Susie flew off the rocking chair and went over to the picture window. "Mommy, they're on our street and I think they're stopping at Mr. Staller's house."

All four gathered about the window, pushing the Colonial-style bows to the side. The ambulance was trailed by a fire truck, and a police cruiser followed up the rear. They were moving together like an incoming three-ring circus.

Joliana hurried to the mud room and tucked into a warm jacket, adjusting her still soggy boots. "I'm sorry that I was only able to tell you part of what's going on. There's something wrong with Grandpa, as well as with Geraldine. I believe that she is hurt, and I must go meet with the medics."

"Mom, please let us come and help you. We're not babies, you know."

Jolianne looked over at the three sets of eyes, so hopeful, so eager. Yes, they were growing up, but she couldn't subject them to danger. She smiled her most in-control Mom smile and said, "By all means, you can help. Brad, I want you to call your dad and tell him what is going on and have him meet me, okay?" Joliana then turned and tapped her oldest daughter on the shoulder. "Karen, have Brad watch Susie for a while, and you go check on Grandpa. He hit his head earlier, so see if he is okay." She didn't wait for a response but instead unhinged the old latch from the door and ran out.

Chapter Twenty-Four

"Officer, officer," yelled Joliana as she ran down Windslow Street. "Please, let me show you!"

The policeman with the scruffy gray ponytail and matching eyebrows turned and eyed Joliana with curiosity. A shadow of disdain quickly crossed from pupil to pupil. Did this man know her, and if so, why did he show such dislike? Joliana had lived in this town all her life and had never known anyone who had shown such an outward aversion to her. However, she was sure that she had seen this classic police vehicle before, resplendent in its old styling and special pumped-up tires. It must have been some car in its prime, but this officer had somehow kept it on the road.

"What can I do for you?" asked the bohemian-styled cop in the most polite of tones.

Joliana stood straight, her leather-booted feet anchored in a drift along the side of the road. A moment ago, she had detected a huge dose of malice, but now this man seemed quite cordial, almost kind, to her. Had she imagined it? Joliana couldn't figure it out, but something did not seem quite right. "Yes, you can help. I'm the one who called. I'm Joliana Faracelli, and I called emergency because I saw a neighbor, Ms. Pryor, lying on the ground. I went over to her and checked on her, and she wasn't moving. I think she was pretty hurt." As Joliana relayed her story, she ambled to the side of the house where, just minutes ago, Geraldine Pryor had lain.

Joliana halted like a deer that was mesmerized by oncoming headlights.

There was no sign of Geraldine. Where she should have been, there was a heaping layer of snow. Incredulously, Joliana surveyed the area. Not only was the indentation of Geraldine's body gone, the circles of boot tracks and

Boomer's paw prints had vanished as well. Joliana trudged through the snow, to the other side of the brush. Maybe she had been mistaken and had walked them all to the wrong side.

"Mrs. Faracelli, what exactly are you looking for here?" Jerry stared hard at Joliana, tapping his boot in the snow.

"A very hurt person. She could even be dead by now," said Joliana. Someone must have found Geraldine and Boomer. Where had they gone?

"Well, Mrs. Faracelli, as you can see, there is no one here. These kind of false calls are a very serious offense; you caused the entire department to come out for a hoax."

"Sir, I did nothing of the sort!" Joliana shouted. She would not be pushed about by this hippie of a cop. "Just a few minutes ago, Ms. Pryor lay here, hurt. I don't know where she could be, but she must be close. We have to find her!"

Jerry swayed his head to his left. A second cruiser had pulled up. A young policeman stepped from the shiny cruiser. "Hey, Jerry, what's going on here? We've got the whole ambulance crew down the street!"

Joliana ignored the exchange and instead retraced her steps. She had been right the first time. Bending down, she looked at the lumpy snow that had replaced her friend. There had to be some clue. Off to the side, there were pieces of lettuce and a ketchup-laden bun. Surrounding the remains of this burger were dog prints, which circled about and headed into the woods. Boomer. He had been coaxed away by one of his favorite foods. But what about Geraldine? Then she saw something: perpendicular lines that met and created block-like forms. They were fashioned not by nature but by some sort of shovel. "Sir, I believe I found something here. Please come over," said Joliana as she waved her arms.

The rookie officer approached her while Jerry trailed behind. "Am I to understand that you are Mrs. Faracelli, the wife of Mr. Tony Faracelli?" he asked harshly.

Joliana stood from her stooped position, an icy tingle plummeting down her spine. "Yes, I am, and I called to get help for my friend."

"Do you and your husband own the three dairy marts in this area, including the Marty's Complete?"

"Yes, we do. Well, really we are part owners with members of the family and ..."

"Well, I have here a report that requires that you come in for questioning regarding involvement in a robbery at that store." The officer spoke in a monotonous manner, his face showing no emotion. Behind him, Jerry smirked, the wrinkles in the corners of his eyes in smiling form.

"Why would you have to question me? I have done nothing! Why would I want to rob one of own stores? It just doesn't make any sense!"

"You can just tell that to the people at the station," said the cop as he moved toward Joliana, ushering her towards the police vehicle.

"But what about Geraldine Pryor? While we're sitting here talking, she could be in fatal danger!"

"Mrs. Faracelli, as you can see, there is no Geraldine. I don't know what you're doing here, but if you're trying to distract us, it won't work. Now, if you would please cooperate and get into the car."

Joliana felt like she was being smothered. What was going on here? She had no time for games! Her vision was tunneling and all she could see were the two policemen standing by the squad cars with a kind of burnt paper edging surrounding the scene. The panic attack was beginning when she saw it. Leaning alongside Jerry's car was a familiar shape. Joliana squinted hard. She was right. It was an old steel shovel that was still wet.

Locking eyes with the younger officer, Joliana frantically pointed her gloved finger. "Sir, sir, look over there by the other car. I believe that that shovel …"

The policeman turned his head towards Joliana, but his gaze appeared to go by her, into the distance, and then he became clearly agitated and beckoned to Jerry. What was going on? This shovel would certainly be key evidence that she was not creating a huge tall tale. Then she saw what the two officers were excited about: a bright streak of mandarin and copper licked the evening sky, and embers fell about like a fireworks display. Lizzie's house was on fire. The fleet of emergency vehicles sprang into action. The fire rescue team hustled about with their hoses. The younger officer hung over the side of the squad car, making calls for backup, and Jerry was hidden by the expanse of his trunk as he rooted about inside. Neither one was paying any attention to her.

She knew a wrapped present when she saw it.

Joliana walked briskly from the chaotic scene. But she did look back, just once. The seasoned steel shovel was gone.

CHAPTER TWENTY-FIVE

"You know, you can't hurt me! I know that you just dumped Geraldine in that corner and covered her with a bunch of rags. You hurt her bad, and I won't let you get away with it!" said Lizzie as she pointed to the far end of the basement, her lips drawn into a surly grimace. She had been tightly secured to the chair. Her limbs were mummified about her, but she had use of her voice, her whining, irritating voice, since, for some reason, she had been bound but not gagged. A throaty groan came from the direction she had been pointing to. "You see, there she is. My good friend, and she's alive!"

"I can't believe what a snoop you are. When I saw you near that window, I didn't know you had seen …" Pete hurled a look of disdain at Lizzie as he toppled over one box then another and kicked at the piles beneath his feet. "You're one crazy woman, and I warn you, stay out of my business."

"Are you planning to cloister me here forever? You know that Hank Staller will be home soon, and he won't like that you're snooping around his stuff. What are you looking for, anyway?"

"Shut up, you crazy woman!"

"Well you can't keep me for long. I've got to take all my pills or I could get very sick. I need my Zyprexa and my Lithium, as well as my daily vitamins. If I get ill, it will be because of you!"

Lizzie paused and waited for a reaction. There was none. Pete kept his head down as he ransacked everything he could get his hands on. "You know, I could get all shaky and turn blue and fall down dead if I don't get my medicine. Then you will have two people to have to answer for!" Lizzie's indefatigable persistence was worthy of a medal.

"You think it's all about you, don't you! But you don't get it. I could care less about you. I just want you to shut the hell up!"

Lizzie was fueled by Pete's caustic mouth. She would not be told to keep quiet. "So what's so important that you attack Geraldine, bind me, and then demolish this basement? Could it be money, some sort of treasure? You know, that there's been rumors over the years that Hank was involved in a bank heist, that there's money hidden. In fact, I remember that a few years back there was a huge robbery at the bank in town. There were two men dressed in superhero costume; well, they claim that there were three, but only one was caught. His name was, um, Peter something. Yes, I recall Peter Smalz. Hey, that's you, isn't it? You're that Peter guy, and you went to prison for an interminable time. In fact, I just heard on the radio that some prisoner just escaped. That was you, wasn't it?"

Pete stood very still. Then he bent and grabbed a short plank of old wood and threw it at Lizzie.

Lizzie thrust her body to the side to avoid being smacked by the spiky piece of wood with rusty nails jutting from it. She let out a howl that would have unnerved the bravest of Halloween pranksters. "You know that I'm right. You and your cohorts were up to no good, and now you've come back looking for the spoils. Anytime now, your friends, Hank and Joe, will show up, unless you've got them all tied up as well." Lizzie sniffed the air like an ambitious scout dog, and her lip curled up.

"You know that you stink. You smell all smoky, like my dirty oven, and a bit like gasoline, too. I wonder why."

Pete turned and angrily stepped over boxes to reach Lizzie. Raising his hand over his shoulder, he sliced through the air as his knuckles rapped the arch of Lizzie's cheek. "Shut up, you woman! Enough of your meddling! Such a foolish woman you are, using freaky memory on me. I think it's time to shut that trap of yours." Pete surveyed the trashed basement and noticed a very discolored wicker clothes hamper. "Ha! Maybe there's something in here to gag you with," said Pete he lifted the creaking lid.

"Did you hear that?" said Lizzie.

"Hear what?"

"There's someone outside. I bet someone's come looking after me. Maybe the police."

"You had better hope it's not the cops." Pete then halted his activity and stared hard at Lizzie. He cocked his head and motioned for her to keep quiet. Lizzie pouted her smeared ruby lips, but Pete jammed an oily rag between her teeth and secured it behind her matted head. Then he edged closer to the passageway to have a better look.

Someone was scratching at the basement door.

Pete inched his way to the badly peeling entry, moving like a skilled predator ready to embrace his prey. He grabbed an old baseball bat with his favored left arm, and with the other, threw open the door and whipped the makeshift weapon at his unseen opponent.

"Hey! What the hell! Pete, it's me Jerry!" The stunned officer then rallied with fists and fended off his assailant with quick body movements.

Pete let the bat drop to the floor. "Jerry, is that you? I can't believe it! You're still with that crooked police station?"

"That was some greeting, Pete. After all these years, you could have at least whacked me in the head a couple of times," he chided sarcastically.

"Well, my hat is off to you, Mr. Police Officer. It's quite impressive that you have stayed on all these years with your crazy antics and sticky fingers." Pete gave Jerry a critical look from forehead to boot toe. "Hey, you've kept that cowboy look, which I understand is quite the fashion nowadays, and the old man gray doesn't look too bad in that ponytail."

"Always trying to butter me up! You're so smooth. Flash the cheese so you can catch your rat. But I'm not falling for that, got it?"

"It's just that I'm in town only for a few days. Maybe if you help me, I could make it worth your time." Pete said attempting an apology, but it had the nuances of a crooked car salesman's pitch.

"Yeah, and would that be like the last time? You promised me a bundle, but I only got the crumbs. Believe me, I wish I hadn't been your patsy. I was taken for a fool."

"Hell, Jerry, I did time! You may have covered for Hank and Joe, but me, I was left to rot!" Pete's large eyes bulged, and his muscled arm seemed to expand right through his sweatshirt. "I didn't get a stinking dime! But I'll tell you this: when I leave here tomorrow, I'm taking my share if I have to hurt someone to get it! So like I said, if you want to stick around, I will hand you a nice wad of dough—that is, if you trust me."

Jerry's thick, salt-and-pepper brows knitted together as he pondered the offer.

Something then crashed in the room, followed by a ghastly wail.

"What the hell was that?" shouted Jerry. Not waiting for a reply, he headed towards the area of the cellar, where the piercing screams were emanating from, and turned towards Pete and chuckled. "So what do we have here?"

"Don't you come near me, neither one of you horrible, despicable men! I was right. You were in cahoots at that bank robbery, and now you've back for the treasure. But you won't get far, because now I can tell on you!" Lizzie scrambled from the floor and darted towards the door, grabbing crumbled newspaper clippings and jamming them in her pockets.

Pete and Jerry attempted to grab at her threadbare housecoat as it flew past them. But Lizzie was way too fast. Jerry bumped awkwardly into Pete, sending him into a pile of boxes. The two men recovered quickly, but unlike a television drama, when they reached the cellar door, Lizzie had disappeared onto smoke-filled Windslow Street.

Chapter Twenty-Six

Pete groaned. Daylight had dipped quickly, creating a violet sunset with crimson overtures. It was a magnificent scene for the ardent photographer, but Pete could care less. All he knew was that it was getting dark and the wind chill had picked up. He was knee deep in a wintry mix of snow and ice and not liking it a single bit. He plowed deeper into the forested area and had no idea what to do. His plans had been foiled. By this time, he should have retrieved the bank roll of money that was clearly his and then found his way out of this crazy town. But that was not to be. Right now, that damn Windslow Street was swarming with cops and emergency vehicles trying to contain that house fire. There was no way to continue his unannounced visits so that he could finish his business. He would just have to hole-up somewhere until morning. Pete tripped over some branches, and the sharp cracking of dry wood shook him from his meandering thoughts. Cursing the tree and all its many buddies, he adjusted the army blankets under his arm and repositioned the flashlight, glad that he had quickly lifted these items from Hank's basement. Pete stood very still and listened. He was out of earshot of all the chaos going on in the neighborhood, but he could hear something, something familiar. He chuckled. It was a sound he had heard in his younger years in a moment of childhood bliss. He saw himself running a kind of obstacle course through the woods with his friends. They would then pause to skip stones in the creek or catch minnows with a makeshift fishing pole. When exhaustion overcame them, they would fall into the soft grass in a small clearing, quieting themselves so they could hear it. Yes, there it was again. Through the tops of the aged evergreens came a delicate sound that imitated a kind of eerie tune. It was known as Whispering Pines. Pete closed his eyes and listened more intently to the wail of the trees. He then turned and redirected his steps, the thin, yellow beam from the old flashlight lighting the way. He had a good hunch he knew where he was.

The club house. He had found it in just minutes and had almost fallen into what was left of it. The single-dwelling lean-to was comprised of odds and ends foraged from every basement and back lot of hardware stores. Pete and his friends Hank and Joe, and a few others he couldn't remember, had used decent wood and roofing materials in a variety of shapes and colors, which gave a kind of odd patchwork quality to the house. Their hard work and diligence had paid off, for the finished product had given them respite from heavy rain showers as well as the steaming sun. However, in the darkness of the forested area, with only a sliver of moonlight, the treasured lean-to appeared to be an odd configuration. It was covered with hardened ice and snow, its precise details masked by nature's pearl blanket.

"Damn," said Pete aloud. This was a place for nice memories on a summer's day, but what good was this hut now? Pete eyed the dwelling with disgust and caution. So this is what he got for all his trouble for breaking out of that hole, for taking all the blame, for being the fall guy. His reward was an icy igloo. Maybe he should just take himself down the street and find a barn with at least some warm hay to snuggle into. Yet that option would be risky. This area was so remote; no one would find him here except possibly a passing wandering creature, and he could handle that. Hell, he could handle anything after the life he had in the pen. That cell had hardened his will and his ways quite nicely.

Pete searched for the plywood door but there was absolutely nothing left of it. Instead, a large branch had been jammed to secure the dwelling and perhaps add a bit of camouflage. Pushing the full tree limb away, he gingerly walked about the single room. The weakened beam of the metallic flashlight carved a thin stream of light into the murky darkness. The bit of moon was gone, as well as the reflective quality of the snow. Pete rubbed his eyes so he could acclimate himself. A stale, musky odor permeated the room, with a hint of something he couldn't quite identify. He felt an odd lump underfoot, and he bent over, aiming the flashlight downward. He figured it to be a rock or another twig of sorts. It was neither. With his scruffy boots, he kicked at the lumpy ground. Believe it or not, he was looking at faded yellow wrappings with the well-known double arches: McDonald's. The flimsy containers still contained remnants of a hearty feast of fries and cheeseburgers. He could almost swear that he could still smell the mustard. He then aimed his failing light at corner of the room and noted other tossed-away wraps. "Damn," Pete said aloud, "this club house not only has new members but has enjoyed some serious party time." A large cardboard box, secured with masking tape, caught his eye. Pete tore at the wrappings and fingered the contents. "Yes!" Things were definitely beginning to look up. It was like discovering a pirate's secret stash. Inside the dilapidated carton, Pete discovered boxes of Twinkie cakes, his favorite since grade school. There was also a sleeve of bagels and a huge jar of peanut butter. There was a bottom layer of canned goods and even a rusty can opener. He had certainly found a pot of gold. Pete dug in. The frozen bagels gave him ample leverage for scooping into the peanut butter, which he attacked like a bear sinking into a honeycomb. The vanilla cakes he saved for dessert, chomping heartily into the frozen delight. Now he was thirsty. Was there anything that might wet his raspy throat and peanut-covered lips? With both hands, he explored the brown box and felt around like groping blind person. Wait a minute, what was that? It was a plastic bag containing something wet and mushy. Pete pulled out a handful of the questionable matter and chuckled. It was a composite of decaying crab apples and cherries, the kind he used to find at crazy Lizzie's house. The current residents must have discovered her orchard as well. Pete hunted again. He pulled out can upon can of cola, which had become so icy that the tin encasement had begun to bulge. The last one had not quite hardened. He quickly opened it and enjoyed the way the slushy cola sat on his tongue. Delicious. Now it was time for a nap. Having stood all this time, Pete grabbed the army blankets and arranged a makeshift bed on a pile of dry newspapers. He then cut the flashlight off and sat in absolute blackness. Pete's body began to relax. He hadn't realized just how tired he really was. His eyelids, itchy and heavy, began their descent. Pete was falling asleep in an awkward Indian-style position, in this rudimentary place in the middle of nowhere. Yet Pete was used to it.

"What do you mean, you're finished? They still look like crap to me."

"But, Mom, I tried. I even used a toothbrush to get at the corners."

"Yeah, the hell you did," said the angry woman, her eyes ponds of molten ink. Then, with her muddied shoe, she kicked the Venetian blinds so hard that several of the slats bent and hung in awkward positions. Then she slapped the red-haired boy in front of her. Pete sunk again to his knees, attempting to scrub the yellowed binding that secured the blinds, as well as wash off the mud spatters that his mother had slung.

"You know what? You're damn hopeless, that's what! I've raised a good-for-nothing kid who can't do anything right! Just look at you. You're so scrawny, with those huge klutzy feet and a face full of pus-filled pimples! You'll never grow up or amount to anything!"

Pete then reached over and grabbed another blind and tossed it into the tub. He continued to scrub with such violent motion that the blinds screeched and wailed against the bathtub surface, putting deep scratches in the ceramic surface.

"Crap! Don't you know what you're doing! Just look at those awful gouges you've made! For crying out loud, don't you know how to clean anything?" With a single Herculean swing of her arm, Pete's mother grabbed the gallon bottle of bleach and poured it on the Venetian blinds. The bleach danced and splattered, bouncing off the metal blinds, creating a noxious spray.

"Hey, what are you doing?" Pete's reflexes were a bit slow, causing the bleach to burn his hand. He tried to take a breath, but his chest felt heavy and his nostrils were stinging. "Why, you burned me bad!" Pete said excitedly as he jumped up from his squatting position.

Long fingernails, exquisite with their oval shaping and crimson polish, swept harshly across Pete's cheek, leaving trench-like gashes. "Just where the hell do you think you're going? You haven't finished the job yet."

For a moment, Pete was too stunned to speak. He stood still very still, like an actor in freeze mode. Then a huge wave of venomous rage rose from his chest, and his ragged nails dug deep into his clenched hands. He had had enough! Enough of this awful servile life and this terrible abuse! Enough of this wicked, vile woman, who was supposed to be his mother! *Enough!* Pete then stood up to his mother, all five feet of him.

"You damn crazy mother, get out of my face! I will not be treated worse than an animal! All you do is spitefully attack again and again, and I take it again and again. But no more! You'll have to find someone else to be your slave!"

"Shut up! No child of mine will speak to me in such tones. You just wait till I get my hands on you!" With a single swoop, she removed her heavy belt and lunged towards Pete.

Pete was way ahead of her. He ducked and used fancy footwork to avoid the whiplash of the belt. Then, eyeing the bottle of bleach, he grabbed it and flung it at his mother.

"Ugh, are you insane? You just wait," ranted Pete's mother, spewing a mouthful of spit and foul words. Her long piano-fashioned hands covered her face as she moaned in pain.

Pete wasted no time. In moments, he was out the door. He sprinted down the street, and he didn't stop for a long, long time.

Pete stirred. Wow, his head ached. That was some dream. His hands were terribly icy, so he placed them close to his mouth and blew on them. The woolen army blankets had fallen from his right shoulder, and he shivered as he rewrapped himself. Pete rubbed his eyes and then continued to massage his face. Just where was he, anyhow? This place did not have the same odors as jail. Then he remembered. As his eyes adjusted to the surrounding shadows, he knew he was in the club house. A sliver of morning light edged its way into the makeshift aperture, flitting on the discarded soda cans. Pete threw the gray and black bedding aside and stood up. Gosh, he was so cold even his breath seemed to be spawning icicles. He had had enough of this sorry camp. It was now time to finish what he had come here for.

It had taken what seemed like gold-sifter's patience to get the kids tucked into their comforters. As Joliana watched their chests crest up and sink down, she hoped their dreams were full of frog ponds, jump ropes, and shopping outlets, not neighborhood fires where folks are burnt like crispy toast. Tony had finally surrendered to the night sheets, and his snoring was echoing from the high ceiling to the bare oaken floors. But not Joliana. It was as if she had downed ten cups of full strength, steeped tea with extra sugar. In her ballerina slippers, Joliana negotiated the creaky stairs with ease. She headed into the living room and lifted up the curtain. The source of the droning white noise was noted; two emergency vehicles remained at Lizzie's place. The rest of the cavalry had gone, leaving a precautionary back up in case of additional eruptions. Joliana wiped the damp window pane with the sleeve of her pajamas, attempting to get a better look.

There was a single light still on at her father's house. The heavy drapes in the side den muted the lamp somewhat, but it was on, meaning that Joe was still awake. He was always frugal and would never leave needless electricity on in the house. Why, sometimes he would even carry a light bulb from room to room. The commotion in the neighborhood had probably been too much for him, as well. Maybe he was angry with her for not returning to check on him or even calling, but she had been so distracted. Besides, if she had attempted to cross the road, she could have spent the evening at the police station. She could call him now, yet she really wasn't in the mood for an altercation. Joliana played out the conversation in her head.

"Dad, are you okay? I mean with the fire and your fall today, I was just wondering."

"Yeah, and you finally decide to call me in the middle of the night? I could be dead and buried, and what would you care? Damn, that fire could have been my house."

"I'm sorry you feel that way. It's just that …"

"It's just what? Damn, Joliana, it's always something with you. Where's a daughter when you need her?"

"Dad, it's complicated. There's so much going on. My head has been spinning."

One of the emergency trucks was grinding it gears as it sped up the street, jolting her thoughts back. She moved from the window, letting the lacey curtain fall. No, now was not a good time to call Dad. She would wait until tomorrow.

Chapter Twenty-Seven
THURSDAY

The smell of a hundred chimneys blasted Pete's nostrils. But he knew it wasn't that at all. It was that crazy broad's house, Lizzie. Positioning a branch near him to maintain his cover, Pete's assumption was confirmed. The cozy bungalow no longer boasted a roof, dormers, or bedrooms. The first floor left a charred remainder of the living room and kitchen. He had always heard that this Owens' woman had stashed newspapers and stuff up to the ceiling, which probably had made for good kindling. Emergency people were still there, and although it looked like they were almost finished, he moved farther back.

He pioneered his way through the dense thicket laden with ice and hardened snow. He drew in a deep breath and released a full vapor trail, like that of a jet. It was arctic cold, the kind of frigid air that had settled in every tree trunk and burrow and was here for the long haul. Pete was not alarmed. He loved the way the wind bit at his cheekbones and pelted the back of his knees. He felt a newfound freedom here in the woods, which he had missed all those years he was caged up. But as tough as he was, Pete was not stupid. He knew that such temperatures would lead to frostbite very quickly. So he had taken precautions before he left the club house. In the snug room, he had found a red and black kerchief, which he had wound about his red hair and elf-like ears. He happened on extra socks, so he put doubled layers on his feet and used the extra to act as mittens. Pete pulled the excess material of the oversized jacket that he had borrowed at Joe's house over his hands for extra warmth and worked the collar close to his exposed neck. He hustled along, figuring that he was getting closer to Hank's place. He scouted a thick pine tree and some brush to hide behind. It was the perfect spot. He could see the house and, more important, the driveway, as well. So far, both vehicles were in sight; the vintage rusty pick-up and the sixties-style white van were still planted in the driveway. Pete settled himself in to wait. Clearing the snow off a nearby stump, he perched himself and then dragged out the last Twinkies cake pack from his pocket.

A door slammed, and boots crunching snow echoed in the yard.

"Get yourselves in the van, right now," said Hank in an irritated voice. "We don't have all day."

"But I thought we were taking the truck," said Bette.

"Yeah, the truck could haul the big stuff much better than the van," added Darcy.

"Well I say that we are taking the van, and that's that!"

"But, Uncle Hank, don't you see …"

"Will you both shut up? The neighborhood is listening," said Hank.

"I don't know why you are so bothered about everything. Why, I …"

The voices stopped abruptly as the sliding door swished shut. The van engine was slow to catch but then revved loud enough to annoy even a hearing-impaired person. Right about now, lacy curtains were being lifted and eyes were staring. Pete fashioned his crooked six-year-old grin, the one that meant mischievous behaviors were coming.

It was time.

Pete bolted from his wooded cover, embracing the stealth of a cougar. He tried the back entry, but it was tightened like Fort Knox. He stomped over to the gray hatchway he had used yesterday and pulled on the rusty handle. It gave way. In moments, he was in.

The basement was dim, the sole lighting being the thin streaks of sunlight that attempted to pierce the filthy cellar windows. He surveyed the upheaval from the day before and decided to pull out the flashlight he had lifted from this place and squeeze out the remaining battery power.

From trudging through knee-high winter precipitation, he was now plowing through piles of a man's precious junk. The fading glow of the old flashlight dipped and swayed to accommodate his search. Where had he forgotten to look? Damn, all that bank money had to be somewhere in this house. Pete came upon the corner of the basement, where an array of blankets were scattered about, the place where he had heaved his overweight package, Geraldine. But she was not there.

There was a loud crash overhead.

Pete remained still, his head cocked, his ear just waiting for more.

It was quiet, like nothing had happened.

Had he imagined it?

Pete made his way up the rickety stairs, softly but ever so swiftly. No creak or noisy footstep would betray him. Once on the landing, he carefully pushed open the door and peered into the kitchen. The room was awash with sunlight and filled with the wonderful smells of breakfast. No one was there. In moments, he was standing on the dingy black and green linoleum, chuckling. He had found the source of the commotion: there was an overturned cardboard box that appeared to have fallen off the table. With his left foot, he sorted the spilled items: hair-coloring stuff, shampoo and conditioner, brushes, combs, and even a scissor. Gosh, he never knew that Hank was into hairdressing. Interesting.

As he continued to survey the table, Pete's eyes opened wide. There before him was a scrumptious feast just waiting for knife and fork. Hank and his guests had left it practically untouched. Abandoning all manners, he swooped down, like a hawk upon its prey, and scooped scrambled eggs, bacon, and sausage upon uneaten pieces of toast and swallowed. He repeated this primal dining until all the plates were emptied and his belly full. It felt good to finally be satisfied. Now for something to drink. Pete ambled over to the stove, where the coffee sat in a small saucepan. He picked up the handle and took a long swig to wash down that wonderful breakfast. He stopped and spat the viscous liquid, heavy with coffee grounds and egg shells, against the wall. Pete swiped his mouth with his oversized red plaid shirt and gave the stucco wall a disgusting look.

"It's time to find my money, so I better begin this hunt," he said aloud, as if speaking to someone. The verbalized thought melted into action as Pete threw open cabinet upon cabinet and every closet and drawer he could find. No nook would be left unvisited. This time, he wasn't leaving until his pockets were full of Grant bills.

But someone had heard Pete's comment. Geraldine. As Pete came closer to the bedroom, she retreated into the dusty corner of the closet and surrounded herself with woolen dresses and furry coats. She would need to be ever so quiet, like a knick-knack perched on her curio shelf.

Chapter Twenty-Eight

"Well all those emergency people are finally gone," said Bette.

"Yeah, with the exception of that one cop, you know, with the gray ponytail. He's probably making sure the fire is really out," said Darcy.

Hank smirked as his hands deftly handled the wheel of the car. "Yeah, good ol' Jerry. You can be sure that he is interested in more than that fire."

Bette ignored Hank and played with the golden charm bracelet on her wrist. "Gosh, it's sad that lady's house burned down. What was her name? Lizzie? Do you think that she was in it?" she asked.

"Don't know, nor do I care," interrupted Hank. "That woman was a royal pain in the ass anyway, so good riddance to her. Now all I want to do is to get back on schedule and pay that electronics store a visit."

"But, Uncle Hank, you must be upset with the mess the fire made and the cops all around. Why, we could have been caught," said Darcy.

Hank did not reply. Instead, he began to whistle as he wound the van through the curved back roads, except when he would momentarily ease up and add on to his floor-length list of items he wanted Darcy and Bette to pick up. Then he would lick his mouth in anticipation.

"Well, Uncle Hank, I think we have quite a stash of stuff to get," said Darcy.

"Yeah, Uncle Hank, but what I can't understand is why you want more. Why, with all the loot we brought home yesterday, I would think enough is enough." Bette's upper lip curled in disgust.

"So you think I'm becoming a bit greedy, do you, now!"

Bette's angular, crimson cheeks arched in dismay. "Yes, you are! All you want is more and more!" Bette squirmed in the badly torn back seat. "And why couldn't we have taken your truck. This dilapidated van is falling apart!"

"Well, for your information, this van will hold more, and everything won't be hanging out like a neon light. So get ready, because today we're going to have fun!" Hank adjusted the rearview mirror and winked at Bette. "Now don't you worry. You can pick out what you want."

Bette wrapped her arms about her chest and made crude faces at Hank. Hank chuckled at Bette's antics while Darcy turned in the front seat and shot Bette a hostile look.

"You know, Bette, those frowns don't become you. Right now, you need to be practicing what it's like to be Joliana, like keeping your mouth shut. Maybe you can grab a piece of paper and write her signature a few more times. I think I have a pen." Darcy haphazardly tossed the ballpoint at her friend.

"Yeah, Bette," added Hank, "it would be in your best interest to try to get into your new role of being that Faracelli woman, because we're almost there."

"But I don't want to do of this kind of theft. What is it called, identity theft? We are really wrecking this woman's life and …"

"Will you shut up!" Hank leaned over to increase the volume of the static-filled radio.

"And at this time, no one is exactly certain where convicted murderer Peter Smalz is since his break from the Twin Arches Prison late yesterday afternoon. The public should know that he may be armed and dangerous. An area search is in effect by the local police, and the FBI is on standby to step in as …" The voice of the news announcer drifted off, becoming distorted.

"Who is Peter Smalz?" asked Bette.

"Yeah, who is he and why are you so interested?" chimed in Darcy.

"Didn't I tell you both to shut up?" With his right hand, Hank pounded on the radio to adjust the ancient tuner and restore the reception. With the other, he drove like a racecar driver.

"Uncle Hank, you're going too fast! What's up with you, anyway? You're going to get us all killed!" Darcy's index finger pointed at her uncle, her face positioned close to his.

Hank paid no attention to their pleas. He barreled the beaten vehicle with strict frontal vision, his head seemingly locked in place. Hank wondered about this escaped convict—Peter Smalz the commentator had called him, but to Hank he was just Pete. Gosh, Pete had spent the better of twenty years in the slammer. How had he survived it all? Yet he had always known that Pete had guts. His memory was keen. He could picture Pete as he had last seen him: a man of short stature but boasting well-developed muscle and brawn.

Yeah, Pete had the nerve and the ironclad courage to pull off anything. At the bank heist, he could see Pete's hardened chin set in determination. When he donned his homemade Superman suit, his dogged persistence pierced through his cool blue eyes. It went way beyond courage, to some sort of altered reality. Yep, Pete was the best. He had taken the lead in the robbery with the stealth of a wild cougar.

He had followed along. Now he was no sissy, mind you; it's just that when Pete took to the helm, he didn't budge. So why fight him? He had joined in Pete's single-minded focus, tried to match his fervor. Together, even without Joe, they attempted to pull their caper off. But it had all gone down terribly badly. One of the bank tellers got jittery, so Pete aimed his gun and fired. He had found his way out of there, but Pete became the fall guy. He got nailed good. But now Pete was out. Where would he go? Perhaps to a sandy beach somewhere to drink gin and tonics. Damn, if that wasn't Hollywood thinking! He knew where Pete would be, if he wasn't there already, and that was in his very neighborhood. Why, of course Pete wasn't going anywhere without his share of the pot, the very share he had stashed in his basement. Hank wiped his damp forehead with the back of his hand. They would have to make good time and get back to the house before Pete.

"Uncle Hank!" Bette yelled as she grabbed on to the door handle to anchor herself.

The rusty van came within inches of nose-diving into an oncoming salmon colored station wagon. Hank rolled down his window and gestured rigorously with his left hand and then stuck his head out, the flow of obscenity so thick it seem to ooze from his lips like rancid molasses.

"What is the matter with you?" screamed Bette.

"Yeah, what is up with you, Uncle Hank? You almost collided with that car. You want to get us all killed?" Darcy moved closer to her uncle and elbowed his ribs.

"Hey, that hurts! Will you both shut up and get ready to visit that store?"

"You just want us to listen to you, our almighty leader. Well, you're just a grizzly old man with a lot of body odor. I know about you. When that news reporter was talking, you got really upset and then very quiet. You know something about this convict, that man Peter, and you're not telling us."

"Bette, put a sock in it!" Hank raised his arm and slammed down hard on the wheel.

"Take a right here, a right here," repeated Darcy.

Hank slammed on the breaks and skidded as he jettisoned tiny pebbles everywhere. They had finally reached their destination, the Valley Electronics Store.

No one said anything. Three pairs of eyes stared ahead, to the store window, and they hardly seemed to blink. Yet their chests heaved in nervous anticipation as their manic thoughts spun about in entirely different directions.

Chapter Twenty-Nine

Joliana had stayed up all night, with plenty of hot tea to soothe her shaky nerves. At sunrise, she quickly washed and changed before the kids and her husband clamored down the spiral staircase to get breakfast. She really didn't want Tony to know that she hadn't slept. Besides, she didn't feel a bit tired. But the last couple of hours had been rough. She had really wanted to get on with this day and work matters through. Maybe not the twins thing, but definitely the lost cards and the missing Geraldine and, of course, her father. She and Tony would make made plans to straighten out their messy situation. The tight bands about her chest would let up.

"Good morning," said Joliana, forcing a bright smile as she turned the French toast.

"Boy, Mom, you're awfully happy today," said Brad.

"Yeah, you would think that with our street on fire last night and with Lizzie possibly dead that you would be a little upset," said Karen.

"Hey, calm down. Mom has made a nice breakfast, so eat up quickly so you don't miss your bus," said Tony. He walked over to the double oven and gave Joliana a gentle kiss on the cheek.

"I'm hoping we can get this credit card thing in order today: call the company, visit the Motor Vehicle Department, and get over to see Dad. He has a bump on his head; he said he fell but he may have had a strange visit from someone."

"Joliana, not now!" Tony nodded at the children, who now surrounded him at the table.

"It's okay. I've told them about what's going on. After all, they're part of this family."

"Yeah, Dad, I'm a teenager now and I'm not stupid," said Brad.

"Hey, I'm part of things too," chimed in Susie.

"Okay, okay, we're all in this together. Once you leave for school, Mom and I are going to speak to a few people, make some phone calls, and get this all straightened out." Tony winked affectionately at Joliana and stroked her hand. "Promise."

Joliana gazed at her husband, wanting to believe his affirmation, but she said nothing. She refereed the tooth-brushing and backpack-loading as the kids hustled out to catch the bus. Now she could respond. "Tony, you really think we can straighten this mess out before the cards fall into the wrong hands? We could get into huge debt and our credit will be awful and we could even lose our house and our savings so that our college funds for the kids will dry up—that is, if they don't put me in prison first."

"Joliana, stop it! Get a grip." Tony moved closer to his wife, put his arm about her, and pulled her close. "Now, hon, we've been through so much in our lives. Don't you think we can beat these cards? Please, don't worry. This will all work out, and I believe we'll be the better for it."

"I hope so." Joliana attempted to return her husband's strong embrace, but she was scarecrow stiff. "I know that last night we were all distracted by the fire at Lizzie's, but I'm still very concerned about the police. They were really on my case, and you even said they interrogated you at the mart. Somehow, they believe I'm implicated in all this, that somehow I am the woman on that tape."

"Jo, I know it all looks bleak right now, but I know that you are not that woman. I don't understand why she looks and dresses like you, but there were some inconsistencies that the police didn't pick up on."

"Inconsistencies?"

"Yes. When I studied the tape, I could see that left hand did not show the lovely diamond I gave you, and her mouth was slightly open and I noticed bad teeth."

"A woman that looks like me but with dental problems. That's very interesting." Joliana wondered why that sounded familiar to her. "So did you tell the cops this?"

"Yeah. We are going to settle things now so that the police will have no case."

"What do you plan on doing?" Joliana gave her husband a bewildered look.

"Well, first I am going to contact the credit card company, and I would like if we could visit the motor vehicle department. Then I have a lawyer friend downtown who can perhaps figure out things with the robbery. So let's finish breakfast and get going. Okay?"

"But what about Dad? With all the commotion last night, I didn't go over there. Tony, I really think something is going on. It's not just his usual messiness."

Tony took a long gulp from his coffee mug and nodded. "With all that's happening, you may just be a bit too anxious about things. But if it would help, we will also pay Joe a visit."

Joliana nodded. He finally believed her and was willing to work together. He had decided that they would be most resourceful if they stayed together. Yet the sleuth in her still wanted to snoop at Marty's store, even though she would risk confrontation with the police. And from there, she wanted to hunt about for Geraldine and Lizzie. But she knew that Tony would not go for her plan. Errands—didn't she always have some to cross off her list?

"Honey, I think your ideas are fine. But to save time, how about I run a few chores and go to the Motor Vehicle Department myself? You know that I can't continue to drive without a license. Heck, I shouldn't be driving at all but we have so much to do. Would that be okay?"

Tony nodded as he drained the sugary remains of his coffee. He agreed to visit her dad as well as some people regarding the lost credit card, and she was on her way to secure a new license. Maybe she would also make a quick stop to purchase one of those newfangled cell phones so she could easily call her family. Hopefully, she would worry less about Tony and the kids. And they would worry less about her. Just maybe.

Grabbing her car keys, Joliana headed out in the salmon-colored Volvo. She checked her wrist watch. Almost nine thirty. On the way to the Marty's, she would stop at the electronics store right after it opened. It would be good timing.

"What was that?" Joliana abruptly turned the wheel to avoid colliding with a decrepit white van and a flowing curtain of rose-colored velour. The station wagon skidded to a stop within inches of the guardrail. The loosened bands about her midriff tightened like thick rubber hoses. She could hardly breathe. The passenger door shot open, and in moments, the same rose fabric was sitting next to her.

Lizzie.

"What on earth are you doing here, running around in the street like a crazy woman? Why, I almost killed you! And now you're in my car, and all you have on in this freezing weather is that awful robe and bedroom slippers!" Joliana gripped the wheel, trying to steady the trembling in her hands.

Lizzie took the harsh chastisement in silence. The owl-like sunglasses shielded her face, casting shadows that masked any emotion. She was an awful sight. Her usually unkempt hair was now hanging in filthy tendrils about her face. Her nighttime attire was badly torn; the left side, which had belted her together, was missing. And she was so dirty; grime covered her from her cheekbone to the folds of her pink robe, and she smelled terribly acrid. What was it? A bonfire, that's what it was. From every pore and woven strand, smoke poured from Lizzie. The house fire. *Oh, God, what has this woman been through?*

"We have to get him. Turn around now and go back!" Lizzie's arms flailed about, and she tugged at the driver's wheel.

"Stop that, Lizzie! I'm not moving anywhere until I find out what is going on."

Lizzie placed her head into her lap and initiated a wail that began in deep baritone somewhere in her diaphragm but finished in piercing tones. "My books, my immense library has vaporized. And the special collection of newspapers and magazines is destroyed." Lizzie continued her annoying lament.

Joliana moved a bit closer to the bereaved woman and slipped her arm around the filthy housecoat, attempting to soothe the shivering shoulder.

"Urggg!" Lizzie struggled to free herself.

"What, Lizzie?" asked Joliana, quickly removing her arm. She sighed. This was one difficult lady, full of inconsistencies. The fire had escalated her usual agitation. Gosh, Windslow Street was growing crazies like cornstalks. They were everywhere behind those seemingly innocent white picket fences and clapboards.

"I have to help Geraldine. That malicious man was there." Lizzie grabbed Joliana's shoulder and pushed her forward. "You have to go back and help her. For all we know, she could be dead! Now go!" Lizzie's clenched hands waved about her face.

"Lizzie, get a grip!"

"You get a grip. Geraldine is suffering, and you're stalling. Why you don't believe me!"

"Now wait a minute. I know that something is wrong with Geraldine because I saw her lying in the snow. I checked her vitals, and she was alive but her pulse was weak."

"If you really did see her, then why didn't you help her?" said Lizzie as she squeezed her hands together.

"Let me finish. I covered Geraldine with my coat and supported her head with my scarf. Boomer, my dad's dog, showed up, so I left him to guard Geraldine. Then I went home to call the police. When they arrived, Geraldine was gone."

"That's because you were too late. That nasty man with red hair had taken her away. He threw her over his back and hauled her down to Hank's basement."

"You actually saw this happen? So right now Geraldine is in Hank's cellar?"

"The same place he had put me and tied me up in a chair."

Joliana's neck and shoulder muscles tensed as she gave Lizzie a disbelieving stare. "So he put both of you in Hank's basement."

"Yes, he even hurled pieces of wood with rusty nails at me, but I was able to duck. But look, my wrists still hurt." Lizzie thrust her hands before Joliana.

Joliana noted the angry rope burns and gashes on her friend's wrists and then looked down at her slipper-clad feet, noticing the same bruising on her ankles. While Lizzie was known for tall tales, this time her story was believable and most unsettling.

"Do you know why this man was attacking you and Geraldine?"

"Sure do. It's all about what happened twenty years ago. That man was looking for something that Hank has."

"And what was that?"

Lizzie stared straight ahead, her mouth moving like she was talking to someone, but no words came out. She raised her arms and shouted, "Let's go!" The she pulled out some colored jelly beans, the kind that are special ordered, and popped them in her mouth. She handed a couple of the lint-covered, sticky candies to Joliana.

"Where on earth did you find these?" asked Joliana as she surveyed the disgusting jelly beans.

"There was another man at Hank's. He had a gray ponytail, and some of them spilled from his pocket. I took them from the floor before I escaped."

"The man you saw, that was Jerry. He's been around for many years and some say that he works a bit under the wire. All I know is that he acted very peculiar with me when I tried to get help for Geraldine."

"That's because he's involved, not only now but with what happened years ago."

"And what exactly happened then?"

"As I said before, we have to go, or it will be too late for Geraldine." Lizzie then folded herself into the passenger seat, tucking what was left of the chenille housecoat about her legs.

Joliana started the engine and checked for oncoming traffic. She realized that Lizzie had just closed down; there would be no talking to her now. She would head over to Hank's in a few minutes, but first she wanted to stop, as originally intended, and pick up those cell phones. She knew that Lizzie wouldn't like it, but right now she needed to buy a little time to figure out this revealing information. Joliana checked for oncoming traffic and then stepped hard on the gas pedal.

"Where are you going? Windslow Street is back that way!" said Lizzie.

Joliana ignored the angry pleas of her strange passenger and focused straight ahead, her next stop the Valley Electronics Store.

Chapter Thirty

Hank wrestled with the scuffed-up cart, that was opposing his commands. He gave it a final yank, and the flat carrier came free. "Now just shut up and follow me," he said. Hank plowed down the aisles, pointing to given items and commanding their immediate placement on the cart. His head moved back and forth like he was crossing a busy highway as he checked out every customer. Darcy and Bette had to hustle to keep up with him. Any attempt at conversation was met with an immediate scowl. Hank was most obstinate, but even more unsettling was that his demeanor had hardened and he appeared dangerous and deadly. Scared, Bette and Darcy acquiesced. They wanted to negotiate this or that item, but such bargaining was not on the table. The women mustered their brawn and stacked the top-of-the-line television sets, video cameras, and the essentials for two computer systems, including extra printers and ink cartridges. The items swayed on the metal carrier such that each woman was balanced on each side while Hank commandeered the stash like a pirate at sea. Bette and Darcy made silent signals to each other, and their angry scowls matched their foul gestures. Hank ignored them and angled into the cash-out area, nodding to Darcy and Bette. "Go for it ladies," was all he said as he hustled from the registers.

"Where are you going?" asked Bette. "Just how are we supposed to get all this stuff out of here!"

"Will you be quiet and watch what you're doing? We can do this with or without Hank," replied Darcy.

Bette shrugged.

"It's show time, and you're going to put on one hell of a show," Darcy whispered.

"I'm not an actress, not now or ever," said Bette, her voice a bit above Darcy's.

'Well, right now you are, so let's get this stuff in the cashier's face. Now."

Bette nodded, her face flushed from ear to ear. She sauntered close to her friend, hoping that this purple-haired cashier was nimble at her keys.

The clerk was miserably slow. Petite and slender in her form-fitting jeans, she appeared agile but she moved like the sloth in the Amazon exhibit downtown. Bette looked over at Darcy, who appeared cool and collected. However, Bette was not. Icy fingers were tripping up and down her spine, especially since the checkout lady was wandering about the cart, writing down every item they had selected. It almost seemed like someone had purposely told this woman to work as deliberately as possible, stalling them so that the police would be ready to slap handcuffs on Bette and Darcy.

"Bette, Bette, are you there? C'mon, let's put some of the smaller items on the counter. With this woman, we'll be here all day."

"All right," said Bette as she pulled clumsily at their stash, causing the carrier to tilt.

Darcy moved quickly to the end of the cart and steadied the heavy television carton. "What is the matter with you, Bette? Just leave things alone and go stand by the counter."

The cashier entered all the items, speaking aloud as she went along, mumbling that she did not want to forget anything. Perspiration had formed on Bette's neck and was slowing dripping down into her bra. She fidgeted with her coat and loosened her scarf. She was getting nervous and sick to her stomach. She had to get in the zone and do this thing. Darcy sent her another one of her seasoned "shut up" looks, which Bette loathed. Bette turned and faced the cashier with the fancy French manicure.

"Will you be paying with cash, check, or credit card?"

Bette froze. Darcy elbowed her friend and motioned for her to answer.

Bette tried to speak, but her mind felt clouded over, like a spider had just spun a web. It was stage fright, a kind she had never experienced with their other capers.

"Will you be paying with cash, check, or credit card?" the cashier repeated in a caustic tone as she twirled a tendril of her violet hair.

"My name is Joliana Faracelli, and this will be a charge …. this will be a new charge," said Bette in a robotic voice.

"Well then, Miss Faracelli, you will need to complete this form, and I will have to see two forms of ID, like a license and another charge card."

Bette pulled a black ink pen from her pocket and began completing the abbreviated form. It wasn't complicated, but she couldn't remember the number of the street address or the phone number that she had committed to memory last night. She scribbled out this information hoping the cashier would disregard it. She hesitated when she reached the bottom. The signature. This had to be done just right. Again, the sweat rolled; this time she could feel her hair dampening on the back of her neck. Then the charm bracelet crashed onto the counter. Bette looked over at Darcy but avoided eye contact.

Darcy was rocking in place, checking her watch.

Bette would not be rushed; after all, she was the one on stage. She rooted into her wallet to secure the requested cards, those hot Faracelli cards. "Here you go," said Bette, trying to regain her everyday voice but careful not to smile, not to show her ugly teeth.

The cashier took the cards and the single-page application and turned them around. She placed the form in front of her and tapped her nails on the counter. She looked up at Bette, then back down.

The second hand seemed to freeze on Darcy's watch.

"So you say here that you are Joliana Faracelli."

Bette nodded, her eyebrows arched.

"Well, I have a question for you. Who does your hair? I can see that your cut and color is a bit different than your picture, and it's awfully nice. Tell me where you go."

"Downtown. It's called, um … well, I believe they have changed the name, and I don't remember it just now," said Bette.

Darcy smiled and winked.

Bette loosened the grip on her pen and slid it in her pocket. She hoped everything was set so they could leave. But what was that? She heard a rustle behind her and saw a glimmer of golden hair shaped like her own. Two sets of aquamarine eyes met, large, round, and unblinking. It was a mirror image that hung suspended for merely seconds. Joliana Faracelli was here. Bette snapped back her head and tried to get Darcy's attention, but her friend was anchoring their stash on the cart.

"Well, here are your cards, and your purchases have been charged for you. This form is temporary; you will get your new charge card in the mail in about two weeks. But I just need one more signature on the bottom on this slip."

Bette fiddled in her pocket to retrieve the ballpoint pen and hunched over the desk. That Faracelli woman was watching, so she had better be very discreet. Now what was the matter? She positioned the pen this way and that, but the ink refused to work. Frustrated, Bette pushed down hard, crushing the tip. "Damn," said Bette aloud as the black ink splattered over her hand and the false marble countertop.

"Here, take this," said the cashier, handing Bette another pen. The woman pulled out a paper towel and some special cleaner and began spraying the dirty counter.

"Can't you just wait until I'm finished!" Bette's patience was waning. She just wanted to get out of there.

The cashier held the slip in her hand, her tongue touching her upper lip. "You've got a very bad ink stain here, but it's still readable." Then she opened her register drawer and shoved the paperwork inside. "Thank you for shopping with us today."

Bette grabbed onto the oversized carriage and began to push. Darcy spotted the rear of the load as the women head towards the door.

"Oh, Miss Faracelli, one more thing," the clerk paused as she spoke to her manager.

Bette's stomach leapt into her throat, the remains of her half-digested eggs and toast nauseating her. Hands with whitened knuckles clenched onto the cold metal. Now what was the matter?

"Miss Faracelli, it would be great if, when you come back, you could bring the name of that hairdresser with you. I'd really appreciate it."

"Yep, I'll get back to you right away," replied Bette, knowing full well that she would never show her face back here in this lifetime.

"Bette, what was all that about? I was getting worried that we would get caught," said Darcy.

"Worried? Why, you were not even paying attention half the time, especially when I tried to tell you about the Faracelli woman."

"What about her?"

"She was in the store—actually, right behind us—and you never saw her."

"Are you serious? I didn't see her at all," said Darcy.

"I'm not making this up. I saw her, and she saw me. I wouldn't be surprised if she is right outside this door, waiting to ambush us."

"I don't know what you saw, Bette, but for now I think you should shut up and say nothing to Hank. We need to think this through."

Bette nodded in agreement as they both pushed the cart out to the van in silence.

Joliana could sense the roots of her hair prickle like they did the last time she ran into that huge German shepherd. It was fear, pure and unfiltered.

That's what she had experienced the moment the cashier identified that unknown woman as Mrs. Faracelli. Then that woman looked over at her and they locked eyes for a moment, turquoise to turquoise. It was like looking in a mirror. Joliana's heart was still pounding tribal tones. Had she met this woman before? Was she a relative she had seen at a wedding or some other function? There had to be an explanation. There was another woman dressed in a lot of black clothing, and there was a older man, as well. While she hadn't seen him up close in a while, she knew it was Hank Staller. So these were the three culprits who had taken her cards and were having a party at her expense! How dare they! The puzzle pieces were quickly locking together; snatches of time in the past three days were making sense. These were the women she had glimpsed at the mart, and all the upsets with Lizzie and Geraldine had their roots at the Staller house. She wasn't going crazy after all; it was these awful neighbors with evil intents. A volcanic surge of anger swept through Joliana's body. What she wanted to do was to make a heroine debut by slapping those two women in the face and then laying a surprise punch on the old guy. She would reclaim her identity, and the victory would be hers. Joliana looked down at the wet pavement outside the store. She had bolted. While her mind fantasized about superhero tactics, her body had run to safety.

All that adrenaline wasted. Maybe she should just take herself back and face her imposter. Then she realized that she was holding on to something: two expensive portable phones. Just great. In her haste, she had now added shoplifting to her list of crimes. Some Christian she was. But she couldn't go back in now. She couldn't risk getting stopped, or even worse, arrested.

Joliana hustled to the dirty salmon station wagon.

"So what took you so long?" asked Lizzie as she helped herself to the packages that Joliana had thrown on the seat.

"Lizzie, I believe I understand what has been going on. I saw those two women who have been causing all this grief. They appear to be Hank's protégés, and he has them doing all his dirty work. But there is something that is very troubling: one of the women looks just like me! I mean, it was like seeing my reflection in a store window."

"Bingo!" Lizzie pointed over to a far corner of the parking lot. "Joliana, look over there. Hank and his friends are loading that white van with all sorts of big boxes." Lizzie rolled down the passenger seat window and stuck her head out.

Joliana followed Lizzie's gaze. "I can't believe this. They really bought a haul of stuff, a lot more than I noticed on the counter. And all of it belongs to me; they used my good name and my credit to buy it. But they're not going to get away with it … not if I can help it!"

Before Joliana considered her next step, Lizzie was already out of the car and running over to Hank, her arms flailing about and her mouth spouting a line of vulgarities.

Joliana sat immobilized in the leather seat, staring out the window. That little lady was a tornado to be reckoned with.

"Hank Staller, you're corrupt and depraved! Stealing like this! And I know that you've got my friend Geraldine in that basement of yours, and she's hurt!"

"Will you shut the hell up! You're one crazy woman." Hank then thrust his fist into Lizzie's face. The diminutive woman fell back onto the side of the van and moaned.

Joliana stared in horror. Her hands trembled as she fingered her keys and attempted to start the Volvo. She had to get away from here. Now. Hank turned his head in her direction and scowled. Then he laid another punch on Lizzie's shoulder, and with a single swift motion, he lifted her up and tossed her into the van with all the cardboard, plastic, and brown bag wrappings.

"Enough, you horrible people. You're not going to rob me and bully everyone!" In moments, Joliana was almost touching Hank's cheek, so close she could smell the rank stale tobacco and bacon on his breath.

Neither spoke.

Hank's eyebrow's arched like those of a cartoon villain.

Joliana countered his inflamed stare with the meanest scowl she could muster. She could feel her mouth twitch and a rush of crimson flood her face. She had played the scared rabbit, but no more. Joliana threw her shoulders back and attempted to match Hank's lanky stature. No way was she going to back down. She would show him!

"Well, we'll see about all that. It's too bad you couldn't leave things alone." He grabbed Joliana and pushed her into the van. "Hey, Darcy and Bette, get over here and help." Hank then looked under the rear seat and pulled out pieces of rope and oily rags. He tossed the items at Darcy.

"What do you want me to do with this stuff?"

"What's it look like? C'mon, smarten up. I want you to tie up those two crazies in the back."

Chaos had broken out in the van. Darcy went to work by first gagging the screaming women and then tying their hands. It wasn't easy. It was like being in rodeo, attempting to tie down a nasty bull, except she had two of them.

Meanwhile, Bette just watched.

"Hey, Bette, you take this," said Hank as his calloused fingers flung a shiny object.

Bette's reflexes were quick as she caught the flying metal. She was now in the possession of a compact Smith & Wesson hand gun. Bette held the gun tight, her eyes wide in amazement.

"Now get in the van and cover these two wild boars!"

Bette didn't wait to hear Hank bark his orders a second time. She perched herself between two cartons to keep both Lizzie and Joliana in view. The icy metal of the gun stung her fingers as well as her heart.

"Make sure you cover them good. I want quiet when we drive back to the house. And you, Darcy, you can make yourself useful by driving back the old Volvo. Get the keys from the Faracelli woman and let's make some tracks."

In moments, Darcy lifted the keys from the bound and gagged woman. It was a piece of cake for her. Engines coughed out their metallic cacophony as Hank and Darcy headed out of the lot.

Chapter Thirty-One

Tony stood by the bay window, planning his strategy for the day. Joliana had left nearly an hour ago, and he still hadn't figured out his time. Canceling Joliana's credit card was the priority, but he wanted to do it right. He had met a fellow who was an ace at this thing called identity theft; he would be the one to contact. What was his name? Tony scratched his chin, a peculiar habit he had picked up from his father-in-law. *Mr. Swanson, that's it.* Now to look for his business card so he could call him. Tony began his frustrated search, looking through this pile and that, which he would often justify to his ultra-sanitized wife as his prized collection of stuff. Tony went from room to room, corner to corner, checking out all his piles. Having no success, he took the couch apart, sliding his hand into the deep side pockets. Thanks to his wife's fastidiousness, he found no dust bunnies, chips, or stale popcorn. Instead, he discovered two quarters that he probably lost last night, but then again, no business card. When did he last see it and actually hold it in his hand? Tony remembered. He flew up the polished oaken stairs to the bedroom. Rummaging through the stack of slacks on the chair, he lifted a pair of beige khakis and dipped into the pockets. Success! A happy flush filled Tony's cheeks, giving him that old St. Nick look. However, the cherubic grin collapsed when he realized that the card was so badly soiled with tomato sauce and anchovies that no matter how he turned it, he was not able to make out the phone number and address. Hm ... what were his options? Stay home and wait for Joliana or get going. Tony bounded the stairs and grabbed his coat. He had promised to pay a visit, so now was as good a time as any.

The doorbell didn't seem to be working, so Tony began knocking, first with a slight rap, which escalated into a pounding, shaking the door. No reply. Tony jingled through pennies and recent movies stubs in his pocket and pulled out his keychain. Though he rarely used it, he had a key to Joe's house. He really didn't want it, but his wife had insisted. "You'll never know when it will come in handy," is what she always said. This time, Tony was most grateful as he turned the key and pushed the door open.

"Joe, are you home? My goodness, look at this mess. Joliana was right; you certainly are a slob. But didn't my wife just help you with all this?"

There was loud grunting from the den in the rear of the bungalow. Tony made his way towards the room, through the broken crockery and the strewn clothing. There were all kinds of papers everywhere, a mixture of the Sunday *Times* and household bills. Joe was sitting in a bulky leather chair, which accompanied the cherry desk; papers and stationery items were all around him.

"Hey, Joe, what's the matter with you? Are you okay?"

Joe continued to spew his four-letter expletives, almost sounding like he was speaking a foreign language.

Tony leaned over and nudged his father-in-law on the shoulder.

"Damn you, Tony, can't a guy get a little peace and quiet?"

"Wow! You've got quite a bump on your forehead, and that's some mean shiner on your eye!"

Joe twisted his face away from Tony's scrutiny. "Leave me the hell alone!"

"But, old man, you're hurt." Tony watched his father-in-law pick up the papers and create a makeshift pile. With age, this man had become an indomitable menace. Tony was grateful that Joliana dealt with his stubborn ways; when he had tried to help, it had led to maligning words and bruised fists. But he always hated that his wife had become such a servant to Joe in her care-giving. He wished he could declare his own rules and enforce them to the letter, but he knew Joliana would intervene with that soft heart of hers.

"Well, are you just going to stand there like some kind of lost buck or did you come over for a reason?" asked Joe.

"Yes, I wanted to find out where Mr. Swanson's office is downtown, so I came by to get his number."

"Don't have it."

"But you know him. Maybe his card is somewhere in this mess. I can even help look."

"Don't bother; it's not here. I gave you the only stinking card I had. But I can do better than that; I'll take you there." Holding onto the ledge of the solid cherry desk, Joe eased himself up. "See, I'm good as new."

"Joe, you look awful. I think it might be better if we call the paramedics and get you some help."

"Hell no! No doctors for me! Why is that when I tell you something, you always want to do your own thing? I just told you that I will take you to Hartford to that guy's office. Besides, I've got a couple of questions for him."

"Yeah, sure, whatever you want. But before we go, just tell me what happened here. I've never seen your house like this. You've been burglarized, haven't you?"

Joe watched his son-in-law wander about the ample den. He shrugged and turned towards the hallway.

"Damn! What a blasted shame. They don't make them like this anymore," said Tony as his foot crunched on the broken shards of German beer mugs. Even the vintage television cabinet had been smashed. "Something is very wrong here. Joe, for crying out loud, I'm family; you can tell me."

Joe rooted for his walking stick in the debris, one he had fashioned from a branch taken from the ailing oak tree in the backyard. He steadied himself with the smooth cane and ambled, with a determined gait, to the hallway. He positioned his upper torso just so, his cane pointed towards the back door.

"C'mon, Joe, don't go playing that deaf and dumb game with me. Gosh, think about Joliana. Wouldn't she want to know what happened?"

"My daughter was already here, and she left in a big rush."

"Joliana was here?" a flash of surprise mixed with betrayal flicked through his usually mischievous Italian eyes. "When was she here?"

"Yesterday. She had stopped by for some reason; I forget. Anyhow, she put some ice on my head and gave me the inquisition, just like you're doing now, but then she took off with that odd woman."

"What woman?"

"That one with the gray hair all stacked on her head; you know, the one who sits in that widow's peak and spies on the neighborhood all day long. She was here."

"You mean Geraldine Pryor?"

"Yep."

"Why, that woman hasn't left her house in years, not since her fiancé from the bank was killed in a car accident."

"Well, she was here, and she was really out of it. She was mumbling and talking gibberish. Joliana tried to make her comfortable, tried to sit her down and all. But Geraldine kept hanging on the door knob, so Joliana took her home. You must remember something about this. For heaven's sake, you called yesterday for your wife, and I told you she was at Geraldine's. You had your dander up."

"I remember that, but I thought she was visiting for some reason. She didn't mention that you were all banged up."

"I guess that's the way it is; I play second fiddle in her life. Why she didn't even call me last night or bring a treat over."

"Joe, you really are a case. You know that Joliana cares about you. Why, she's here more often than her own home, and she does so much for you."

"She wasn't much help last night. Why, I could have been dead for all she knew."

"Damn you, man, can you hear yourself? You're moaning like a two-year-old. Grow up!"

A sly smile crossed Joe's face. 'Still haven't answered why she wasn't here."

"I don't have to justify myself to you. But if you were paying attention at all last night, you would have seen our neighborhood up in flames and the entire street packed with emergency vehicles."

"Yeah, I saw crazy Lizzie's place burning."

"I think we should get going to Hartford—now," said Tony in an aloof tone.

"Yeah, it all comes down to how much you hate me. You and my daughter should never have moved into that house across the street. It was a horrible decision."

Tony glared at his father-in-law. Joe was right, dead right. He would like to put his fist into his doughy cheek, that's how right he was. Why the hell they had moved to this windy and long Windslow Street? Because of Joliana. She had loved their Colonial house; even as a kid, she had she studied it from her family home.

Joe zipped up his worn-down parka, feathers trailing him as he followed Tony to his truck. Silently, the two men climbed in and settled themselves on the soft leather interior and headed up Windslow Street. Tensions were heavy. They both sat stoically, as if a steel wall was wedged between them. It was going to be a long ride, thought Tony, as he pushed down on the gas pedal. The truck lunged forward.

"Hey, not so fast. Look over there!" said Joe.

"What's the matter with you!" Tony shoved Joe's hand off the steering wheel. His father-in-law was certainly a one-of-a-kind gem. Maybe they shouldn't bother heading up to Hartford.

"Stop, stop now. Look over a Hank's. Isn't that Joliana's station wagon?"

Tony braked and cocked his head back since he had already driven a bit past the Staller house. Sure enough, there was his wife's car, tucked a bit to the side of the driveway. What was Joliana doing there? They weren't especially friendly with this ornery fellow. Why, the last time he spoke to Hank at all was a brief greeting at the town diner. So much had happened the past couple of days that he didn't have a good feeling about this. Why Joliana was wanted by the police for a crime she didn't do and who knows what else was going on. Tony lifted his foot from the brake and put the truck in reverse.

"What are you doing?" asked Joe.

"We're going to park near these bushes and then have a look around."

"Hank isn't going to like that. He hates trespassers. He'll come after us with a gun, I know it."

"So you're a damn chicken. Don't you want to know what is happening with your own daughter? What kind of father are you, anyway?"

Joe slumped in his seat, stroking the gray stubble on his chin. He made clucking noises with his tongue, sounds he made when he deliberated something.

"Well?"

"You're right. We have to do something. Maybe you could just call the police."

"Police? I don't think so. I just had a confrontation with them that put the entire family in a suspicious light, especially Joliana. I'd say we check this out ourselves."

Joe squirmed in his seat, taking the zipper of his jacket and moving it up and down. "I'll go on one condition: that if it all goes bad, you will call the police."

"That sounds reasonable. Now let's head up this side of the fir trees so we can get to the backyard."

Tony and Joe made their way through the snow drifts, staying close to the cover of the cedars. Finding a crumbling wall of stones, they watched the house.

"Damn, this cold," said Joe as he blew warm air on his fingertips. "I should have taken my favorite gloves."

Tony paid no attention. Instead, he eyed some colorful packaging in the snow and dug for it.

He pulled out what was left of a Twinkie wrapper and an empty cola can. "Looks like this place had been staked out before us," Tony then pointed ahead towards the garage, "and there's even a set of boot prints heading towards the old bungalow, and they aren't ours."

"So what are we doing?"

Tony positioned himself close to the rock structure and winked mischievously.

"Right now, we're going to wait. And watch."

Voices, somewhat muffled by the snowdrifts, came from a rusty van as two women worked steadily to unload the numerous boxes. Hank was there as well, shoving Lizzie and Joliana towards the house. Tony's usually ruddy face went clown white as he watched in horror. He attempted to rise to his feet when Joe pulled him back down. "Not yet, Tony," said Joe. "In a few minutes, I'll show you the better way to crash this place."

Chapter Thirty-Two

"Give me the gun," said Hank as he grabbed the weapon from Bette. "Now help Darcy unpack this stuff into the garage." Bette nodded obediently as she hauled crate and cardboard box into the shadow-filled space.

"Hey, aren't you going to give us a hand?" asked Darcy.

"You two, knock yourselves out and be careful not to break anything." Hank glanced up the driveway and, noticing the beige Volvo, shook his head. "Darcy, what were you thinking? Leaving that woman's car that far up the drive is like waving a surrender flag. Move it, now!"

"I know, but I saw the van here and figured you could use help."

"Shut the hell up! I'm so sick of your 'but this' and 'but that.' Just do what you're told and keep your bad lip to yourself. Got it?"

Darcy shot her uncle a vengeful pout and stood very still for a moment. She walked slowly up the driveway to Joliana's car. She returned to the white van, using her brawn to haul their stolen goods into the smelly garage. She lifted each container with ease and quickly released it, giving no mind to breakage—that is, except for the items she had personally hand-selected to bring home to Pennsylvania.

Hank waved the gun at the occupants in the back seat. "Okay, you two, get out nice and easy, and no funny business, especially you in the dark glasses."

"My name is Elizabeth Owens," said the eccentric woman as she made her way to the rickety sliding door on her hands and knees. A muted wailing emanated from her dislodged gag.

Hank shot Lizzie a disgusted look and turned. "Now you, Ms. Joliana Faracelli, our honored guest of the day, get out!"

Joliana ducked her head and made an awkward exit, considering her hands were still bound and her mouth taped. Looking over at Lizzie, she wondered why that woman always made Himalayas out of everything. The Owens woman could be annoying, but she was also a risk-taker. Just a few moments later, Joliana glimpsed a flash of her velour housecoat as it flew by. Lizzie was indeed fast. However, Hank was faster. His reflexes in place, Hank threw out his free arm and caught the hydrangea blue collar of her pajama top. Joliana smirked. That was one up for Lizzie; at least she had the guts to try to flee from these vile people.

"Lizzie, where do you think you're going? Just because you can run like an athlete, you think you can outsmart me! Well, I'll show you who is boss." Hank nudged the two tone Smith & Wesson into the small of her back and motioned for the two hostages to head towards the old house.

As Hank hastily open the back door, the pleasantly warmed air and the remaining morning smells of bacon, eggs, and something garlicky welcomed them. "Now I want both of you to stay put at the kitchen table," he said as he stuck his head out the door and barked additional directions at Darcy and Bette.

Joliana shuddered and gingerly approached the dirty table. It was laden with pieces of stale toast, runny ketchup bottles, and old newspapers. Granted, it was warm in here, but the place was a mess. She was glad she didn't live like this. Besides food, there many boxes of opened merchandise everywhere, the wrappings strewn about the room. Where had all this stuff come from? She knew. These criminals had helped themselves to the candy bowl at her expense! They had orchestrated this, the three of them: Hank, Darcy, and that other woman, the one they called Bette.

Who in the world was Bette, anyway? She had her hair styled and colored like Joliana's, and she was outfitted in similar clothing. She even wore touches of glamour, lipstick and blush that were the same color palate. But there was something else—that is, except for the horrendous set of teeth that woman had. The woman called Bette looked so much like her, she could even be her. She wanted so much to throw the inquisition at Bette, but her mouth boasted a thick strip of silver Duck tape. Maybe she could be like Lizzie and somehow release herself from these bindings. Joliana discreetly began to twist and wriggle the rope tied about her wrists.

"What the hell is going on here?" Hank surveyed the kitchen, stepping into stray pieces of bacon and broken, mismatched kitchen crockery. A shattered jar of Italian sauce had splattered everywhere, making the place look like an ax murderer had stopped by. The spicy, pungent odor was overwhelming. "We've had an unwelcome visitor; just wait until I find who did this!" Hank again stuck his head out the kitchen door. "You two, come in. We'll leave the rest for later."

Darcy and Bette had paced themselves, becoming a kind of synchronized machine, and ignored Hank's demand. They were almost done. They took their time hauling a cumbersome box that contained the color television they would eventually take home.

"I mean now, ladies, not when the daffodils bloom," said Hank.

Darcy shut the garage door, and Bette heaved the sliding door on the van snugly in place. They sauntered towards the house.

"Did you see that?" asked Darcy.

"See what?"

"I thought I saw something move in the backyard, something blue and red."

Bette glanced over the ample backyard, seeing nothing remarkable. Then her eyes rested on an interesting object. She walked a couple of steps over to investigate, but avoided stepping in the mounds of snow. "I just see some wrappers flying about, that's all."

Darcy shrugged and headed toward the kitchen door.

"Well, it's about time that you two came in! Just look at this place! Hey, watch these two crazies while I check out the rest of the house." Hank left the kitchen and wandered into the den and the small bedroom, his gun pointed and ready. Ugly words and crashing sounds echoed through the house as he added to the chaos.

Darcy carefully stepped over shards of glass and red sauce.

"Gosh, this place was really trashed; even this nice turkey platter is shattered, not that Hank really cared about it," said Bette.

"Uncle Hank, who do you think did this do you? I mean, it looks someone had something particular in mind. They didn't bother with your wife's silver collection or her lovely Hummel figurines," asked Darcy.

Hank did not reply. Instead, he walked slowly up the hallway, towards the sequestered guests, with his hands reaching for the chipped ceiling.

Bette dropped the pieces of the retrieved turkey platter, and Darcy just stared.

Lizzie crouched in a dim corner of the room and folded her robe about her legs such that she was likened to a soft blanket. Joliana rested her freed hands behind her back and decided it would be better to play hostage a little bit longer. Each remained set in her given position, as if posed for an oil painter.

"Everyone up and against that wall, now!" Hank moved towards the yellowed wallpaper, revealing the unwanted visitor, who was brandishing the metal of his own gun. For a man of short stature dressed in attire that was way too big for him, he held a commandeering, no-nonsense manner.

"Now aren't we one happy family, waiting to share a pot of stew and some crusty bread!" Pete laughed scornfully as he eyed each one of his hostages. "Now maybe, just maybe, we can have us a nice party once we finish our business." Pete's angry, violet-and-blue-marbled eyes settled on Hank.

"Now tell me where it is," he said, aiming the barrel of the gun right in Hank's face.

Hank stood rigid against the soiled yellow and green wallpaper. He stared back, unblinking, his face a contorted mask of hatred.

"Answer me! I know you've got it, and since you are so distrustful of banks and everyone else on the planet, the only logical place would be somewhere in this house! Where did you hide that two million?" Pete pushed the gun to Hank's head; his hand held it solidly as if he had been hired as a professional hit man.

Joliana swallowed hard. This was getting way out of hand. The man called Pete was small in stature but definitely determined and tenacious, and very dangerous. She wondered why Hank was standing there and not fighting back. Why, she had seen him slip a gun in his pocket before he surrendered. Couldn't he just pull some of the moves you see in the movies and kick Pete in the groin, whip out his gun, and claim back his house? Not that that would help them; they would still be held at gunpoint. How naïve could she be? Joliana swirled her tongue on her front teeth, figuring out her next move, now that her hands were free. From one corner of her eye, she sensed movement: Lizzie.

"I know where it is!" Lizzie rushed behind Pete, startling him. "It's in the basement in a hiding place that you missed. I know because I watched Hank from the cellar window, and he changed the secret place many times." Breathless and excited, Lizzie then bounded down the basement stairs before he could respond.

"Damn that woman. She's so slippery! So, Hank, is she right? The money was downstairs all along?" asked Pete.

Hank's face hardened, the deeply etched neck muscles frozen as if set in plaster. His eyes appeared as deep ink pools. He said nothing.

"What's the matter, cat got your tongue? Well, I'll just take that as a yes." Pete pushed Hank towards Joliana, bumping them into Darcy and Bette. He waved the gun at the entire troupe. "All right, everyone down to the cellar, slow and easy; no funny business! You go first," said Pete as he poked the gun barrel into Joliana's shoulder.

The disquieted group of hostages made their way slowly into the damp basement.

The heavy boots halted their stomping in the first floor bedroom. It was momentarily still. The attack came swiftly, as if a torpedo had been unleashed. Pete turned over bureau drawers, casting socks and underwear everywhere. He shook out the contents of the desk and emptied the bookcase. Anything in his way was thrown violently against the wall, including the trash can. Prompted by curiosity, Geraldine had left the security of the coats in the closet, and, hunching down, watched the activity through the wooden door slats. She wondered who this small but powerful man was. He seemed familiar to her, but she just couldn't place him. Pete turned and faced the closet. Did he see her? Geraldine wasted no time easing herself into a deep corner of the closet, burying herself in several furs that had probably been the property of Mrs. Staller. She nestled her feet among the many pairs of high-heeled shoes and calico slippers.

Pete was coming closer.

Geraldine took in a deep breath, but she was too late. A horrific panic attack had erupted. The familiar heart racing began, and she could swear that Edgar Allen Poe had never heard such pounding. Her hands were shaking, and her fingertips were like icicles. Sweat was flowing down her back, and she was inclined to throw off those heavy furs but she didn't dare. She told herself to calm down and stop the crazy twitching—now.

The closet door was thrown open, the wooden slats breaking off their slots so they hung at miserable-looking angles. Pete wrestled through the combination of the delicate feminine attire that had belonged to Hank's wife and the smelly plaid clothing that Hank wore. Hangers went flying and various garments began to pile at the man's feet.

"Damn those Stallers! All this pathetic stuff! I know that Hank stashed the loot somewhere, and I will find it!" A sweatshirt-clad arm swept over Geraldine as Pete explored the upper storage area. Geraldine's eyes opened wide, and her mouth fell open. But she made absolutely no sound. Boxes were turned over as fancy hats boasting colorful feathers were tossed and stepped on. Shoe cartons were next. Instead of containing footwear, the boxes held papers of all sorts, which Pete dumped and scattered. Pete mumbled raunchy language as his persistence only turned up dirty parsnips. He grabbed the clothing rack and shook as hard as he could, like Godzilla gone completely crazy. "Damn you, Hank!" He turned and stomped out of the room, kicking anything that was in his way.

Geraldine was as frigid as one of those snow banks flanking her house. She could hardly believe that he had missed her. Was he really gone? Could she move from this furry suffocation? She didn't want to make any stupid moves that would bring that madman back. After all, she was a big lady; well, not fat, but she carried a full figure. She listened intently. She heard one voice, then another, then the slamming of a door and more voices, which were not the intruder's. There was one that she could identify: Hank's. She was sure it was him. Geraldine heard the change in verbal tempo escalate into bursts of shouting.

Geraldine had to look. Her snooping side had won out, overcoming the panic and her feeling of safety of the closet. She tiptoed to the door and stood to the side of it so she could view the hallway that led to the kitchen. She was good at positioning a peeping eye and hiding herself. At least she thought she was. Pete emerged from another side room, perhaps the den, and stuck his weapon into Hank's ribs.

"Up with those hands!" Pete dug the gun deeper into Hank's plaid jacket.

Hank's entire upper torso shook as if hit by a tsunami wave. He acquiesced to his assailant but not before he slipped his Smith & Wesson into his jacket pocket.

"Why, Pete, you've finally got me!" said Hank, recovering from his initial startle. "I'd been expecting to hear from you soon since your breakout is all over the news, but couldn't you have shown a little decency and not trashed my house?"

"Hey, you should be grateful. I gave you the light touch. Now shut up and get into the kitchen," Pete hissed.

Geraldine gasped. Pete. She knew this man. Why, he was one of those fellows who used to fraternize with Joe Willard and Hank Staller. If her memory was at all accurate, Pete had gone to prison for robbing the town bank and murdering a teller in the process. It was rumored that there were three culprits, who had dressed as superheroes and stole two million dollars. Geraldine could feel her heart palpitations pick up. Oh no. All this happened about the time her fiancé was killed in car accident on Route 82. She remembered those costumes; she was there with her husband-to-be when Mrs. Staller was ironing them. The three robbers were Hank, Joe, and this man Pete. What part had her fiancé played? Maybe it wasn't an accident, after all, that her beloved had died. These men were corrupt people and very dangerous. Geraldine began to shake, but this time it was not a panic attack; it was justified anger.

The voices altered in their pitch and seemed to be quieting. Geraldine tiptoed from the room and slid into the den. From there, she got a good view of the queue of hostages heading down the basement door. Joliana was first. This was becoming very bad. She had to get help. Glancing about the room, she noted a telephone that was perched on the coffee table. She scooted over and lifted the receiver. Alas! There was only the sound of dead air, no dial tone at all. Then she knew why. The wire had been cut. So much for doing the right thing. So now what? Making sure the hallway was all clear, she made a dash to the kitchen and was about to head out the door when she heard a creaking on the cellar steps. She ducked into the side pantry and crouched behind two stacked cardboard boxes. Geraldine heard the voices again. They were perfectly clear. How could that be? She pushed aside some stale boxes of cereal and canned beans and noted the origin of the echoed voices. It was the rusty laundry chute, probably once used for kitchen towels and whatever else was dirty. She thought she was the only person in the neighborhood who had one, but she stood corrected. She peered inside the dark metal tubing. Fortuitously, the receiving end of the chute was wide open so that it had become a primitive type of telephone. Very interesting. Then she saw something else. On the wall to the side of the chute was a fuse box that was outfitted with pull latches that turned a circuit on or off. She opened the metallic unit and, to her delight, the switches were all marked with peeling masking tape that labeled each area. She noted the one that said "Basement." As she turned towards the pantry counter, she saw there were several jars of bottled spaghetti sauces, as well as bread-and-butter pickles, so she grabbed one of each. Geraldine had a plan. She would wait until things went way out of control, and then she would throw that switch and dump some surprises down that chute.

"Stand over there in a horseshoe, so I can see you," barked Pete.

Hank, Darcy, Bette, and Joliana slowly took their places. Darcy glared at Pete, the kind of look that would make most people, especially wanted criminals, very uncomfortable. Pete paid her no mind.

His head turned full circle to take in the racket he heard.

Lizzie.

"Oh this is such an imbroglio, but it is all heading to an ignominious ending!" Lizzie danced a queer kind of whirling tap dance as she circled the moldy wicker hamper. "Oh, those opprobrious people, they will get their tar and feathers in the end!" Lizzie then pointed her finger at everyone, except Joliana. Her laugh was shrill and scary.

"What in the world is she talking about?" Bette's mouth hung agape, showcasing her yellowed molars.

"Bette, she's the town's nutcase; and I used to think she wouldn't hurt a flea, but now she's becoming a downright nuisance," said Darcy.

My dear Lord. Joliana shook her head. This was getting very bad. Guns, a hefty purse, and such hostilities were going to make this a perilous situation. She surveyed the room for something she could use as a weapon. She eyed a thick wooden plank that was resting near the wall.

"So, Hank, the stash has been in the hamper. Somehow I missed it. Why don't you do the honors and take it out for me?"

"I don't know what you're talking about. Just look at yourself, listening to that crazy woman," said Hank.

"Now, old man!" Pete pulled up his sleeve and aimed his gun high and close to Hank's callous heart.

"I don't have it."

"You're a liar. I saw you put it there!" Lizzie stood tiptoed, her finger wagging in Hank's face. Her cheeks were flushed, and her bug-like sunglasses hung askew.

Creak! The cellar door was pushed open, giving everyone an unnerving welcome.

Heavy footsteps hit the basement floor and cardboard boxes toppled.

Joe and Tony.

Joliana's eyes opened wide. These dramatic entrances were throwing her hormones into a tailspin. Good heavens, now her father and husband were here, and they had no idea what they had just walked into. And they probably didn't realize that Lizzie had just snuck by them and went out. Pete was holding a gun on everyone, standing with two hands holding the weapon and his legs parted and planted on the cement floor. Joliana remembered this man. He used to spend time with her father, although the image in her mind was still shadowy. What she did recall was an odd but beautiful tattoo on his arm, the same one she saw on this man. It was an American eagle with a full-feathered face that heralded a look of vengeance. Pete used to call this marking his new vision on life: swoop and attack. *Oh, God*, Joliana prayed. This Pete was beyond armed and dangerous.

Pete hustled over to the entrance. "Now, hands up! Stand over there next to the others!" Pete raised the pistol and motioned to Joe and Tony.

"Look at us, finally having a reunion after all these years. Maybe I should go take out my best scotch," said Hank.

"You shut up and do your job by unloading that hamper. Let's see if there's nothing in it."

"Hey, Pete, what the hell is the matter with you? First you rattle me and my house, then you take my gun, but you have a lot of nerve taking my daughter. Look at her; she's all tied up and her mouth is taped," said Joe.

"Yeah, I don't know what is going on here, but if you would just give me Joliana, we'll leave, nice and quiet," said Tony.

"Damn, I'm not leaving until I get my daughter and a piece of what's in that hamper. I did a lot to pull off that heist," added Joe.

"Hell, no!" Hank eyed Joe with contempt and spat in his direction. "You're damn yellow, running off like a puppy dog with his tail between his legs! You deserve a kick in the ass!"

Hank rolled up his sleeves and turned towards Joe.

"Stop there," yelled Pete. His arm then swooped down with the agility of an eagle and swept Bette off her feet. He positioned the gun close to her forehead and held it there. "Now, Hank, what will it be, the money or this sweet woman's life?" Stunned, Bette hung limp in Pete's tight wrestling hold.

Hank snorted from deep in his throat and walked towards the mold-covered hamper. He removed small cartons that sat atop the wicker box. His movements were slow and deliberate.

"Let's go. We don't have all day," said Pete.

"Yeah, let me give you a hand. We can all work together to sort this out," added Joe.

Tony pulled his father-in-law back in the line. "Now, Pete, I don't care what's in that damn hamper. I just want my wife so I can get out of here!"

"Shut up!" Pete's face tightened like he had pulled a nylon stocking over it. "Hank, just get the damn money!"

Hank resumed his task. He flipped the top of the hamper open; it hung on one hinge. He removed smelly pants and shirts and a load of crumbled, yellowed newspapers. He lifted out the tattered, leather briefcase.

"That's it. Now hold it up high so I can see it," said Pete as he edged across the room, dragging his blond hostage with him.

In a perfectly synchronized motion, like that of a Western gunslinger, Hank threw the briefcase at his feet, pulled out his hand gun, spun around, and faced Pete.

"Put the gun down and let her go!" shouted Hank.

"No way. You had better back off or I'll shoot!"

"Well, Pete, if I recall right, when we bought these here guns—that is, bought them all fair and legal out of Jerry's trunk—they were sister pieces, except that one had a little glitch."

Pete gave his gun a long stare and then eyed Hank's. "Yeah, I do remember that one of these guns was wonderfully sweet and had perfect aim, but the other, well, it had a tendency to misfire. After the heist, we were going to dump it along with the gun that killed that woman."

"You mean the teller you killed, right after she loaded up our leather case with money. I never figured why you did that," said Hank.

"Had to. She was acting strange, a bit too sneaky. That's when I threw that Smith at you and told you to get rid of it; then you took off before we were finished."

"As far as I could see, when we were done, I had the gun, which was the evidence, since it was covered with your prints. I grabbed the money and took off," said Hank.

"You were a disloyal jerk, running off and leaving me."

"Pete, you killed a woman; that wasn't the plan!"

Pete's angular face reddened, matching his curly hair, his eyes ready to shoot squid's ink.

Hank continued, "So what I have here in my hand is the very same weapon that wasted that woman, while you, my friend, have the lemon, the one that Joe took off with that day."

Pete tightened his grip on Bette, causing her to wince. She struggled to tear herself from his hold, but Pete only pulled her closer, pressing the gun to her temple. "Shut up or she dies! Lemon or no lemon!"

Joliana watched Bette's muscles tighten as she resisted her captor. Then their eyes met, deep green to deep green. There was a familiarity here. They had never met, but they knew each other. Neither flinched, their eyes unblinking; they stood frozen, caught in a kind of time zone. Mortal danger was the signal between them. The wielding of a wooden plank wasn't just her idea anymore; Joliana would hold out for the right moment and the signal from this woman, her twin.

There was a deep hush in the cellar. The pinging of the furnace was the only sound.

Hank broke the silence. "Pete, it would be in out best interest to work together. We could split the money, and I could help you find a safe place."

Pete eyed Hank with suspicion. "Right, but what do we do with all these witnesses, shoot them all?"

"You and your trigger-happy thumb. No, we can just tie them up real good and then be a hundred miles from here before anyone knows different."

"Tie them, are you kidding? I don't think so. These people are damn sneaky; that strange one with glasses just went out the door. But maybe we could do something." Pete surveyed the basement, and his eyes rested on a corroded, hinged door. "Hank, just what is on the other side of that door, another way to Narnia?"

Hank glanced over to the peeling door. "Could be the way to Oz, but it's really just a cold cellar, where my wife used to store all her canned applesauce, string beans, and hot pepper jelly. I haven't been there in years. I would imagine you'll find a lot of rotten stuff and sticky spiders' nests."

"You, yes you, all decked out in those black clothes, get over there and break that padlock." Darcy sneered at Pete as she began making her way across the room, swearing as she went.

"Hey, we have a live one here. Just use all that spunk to break in, which should be damn easy for you," said Pete.

Darcy found a stray hammer and pounded at the padlock. In moments, the pieces fell to the floor. Then she tugged at the ill-fitting wooden door, finally dislodging it by pressing her knee on it. "Finally. It's open. Are you happy now?" Her tone was bitter and full of insolence.

Tony was rocking in place, his face a hot crimson. He was a missile ready for launch. Joe was right behind him, fuming as he clenched his right hand. Stale air rushed out, heavy with the scent of rot and mold, as Darcy swung open the door. As Joliana watched her family reach their peak tolerance, she could feel her stomach tighten and her breath come in short gasps. She looked over at Bette, who nodded towards the wooden plank.

"Okay, everyone in there, now," demanded Pete, "including you, Hank." Hank's face paled, astonishment turning to bitterness. "Now, throw the gun in front of you and kick the briefcase over to me."

"But I thought we had a deal."

"Hank, you're so stupid, I didn't agree to your plan. Just mind your business and move into that room or I'll shoot someone!" Pete angrily kicked at rakes near him.

"Put the gun down!" Tony charged from the line with his fists up.

Joliana reached for the jagged plank and swung with Herculean strength.

"Don't!"

Abruptly, the lights went out.

The glass jars met the solid dirt flooring and shattered. The savory and sweet smells swirled together. Tomato sauce and pickles.

A shot rang out, its blast deafening every ear. Thud. The bullet found entrance somewhere in the room.

"Oh, no!"

"God, please help us!"

Another shot went forth. Its flight was short-lived as it met its mark, hot metal meeting warm, quivering skin.

War broke out. The front lines were open and vulnerable. Screams bounced off the ceiling and every crevice in the basement. Years and years of junk went crashing and glass shards went flying. Boot-clad feet pounded towards the cellar door.

Then there was silence.

May 1998

Joliana filled her lungs with the delicate lily of the valley scent that was coming from behind her. She headed up a grassy incline and gazed over the flowing inlet of water that was called the Wethersfield Cove. She had always loved this place and had never lived far from it. She would often visit here, no matter the weather. Winter was most enjoyable as she watched all the skaters and ice fishermen, but spring had to be her favorite. Just standing here calmed and soothed her soul more than a warm bath with fragrant herbal salts. This day in May was awesome with the brilliance of the cerulean sky meeting the delightful sparkle of the sun kissing the cresting ripples. Across the water, the view was postcard-perfect, accenting the Colonial housing and leaf-trimmed foliage, which reflected in the water. She was glad that the boaters were not out today as they were on the weekends, when everyone vied for his own wave. Joliana lent her cheek to the sun and felt its warming rays. She was finally herself again. Well, not exactly; she was a refined model. With all the changes of the past weeks, she was hardly the person she was before; she had morphed into someone she liked much better.

So much had happened since that Hitchcockian moment in Hank's basement. Even though many days and nights and hundreds of minutes had passed, she could recount everything with frightening accuracy. That intense scene was always there, still trapped in her mind, unable to find its place in the long-term library of the brain's hippocampus. All she had to do was to think.

That moment.

Twin two-toned Smith & Wessons pounding off their ammo with alarming strikes of thunder. Within seconds, the basement lighting totally went out. And then there was the unnerving crashing of glass.

But right before that, Joliana had kept her gaze on Bette, who continued to be held tight in Pete's wrestling hold. There it was, the sign from Bette: a subtle twitch of her hazel eye as she nodded to Joliana. She immediately grabbed the nearby plank and began swinging. The solid wood smacked Hank dead center in the abdomen. In the scant second before darkness enveloped them, Joliana saw Hank's face dissolve into pain, but instead of clutching his stomach, he attempted to retrieve the fallen gun and money on the cement floor. Hank aimed at Pete as his ally-turned-enemy returned his fire. Then it went dark.

A cacophony of shouting and brazen foul language filled the cellar. Boxes were falling, crystal was crashing, and the tinny sound of lawn equipment added to the pandemonium. Joliana felt a thud at her feet, which was probably Hank as he lurched for the gun. An arm brushed by, nearly knocking her over. Then someone grabbed her shoulder and pushed her towards the basement door. She had to get out of there. Joliana now sensed a prickling in her scalp as she had experienced that day; it was the adrenaline rush that terrorists thrive on. With the others, she had beelined towards the thin streak of light that meant freedom. Her hands were trembling, and her throat had gone desert dry. Outside, even the late afternoon clouds appeared heavy and darkened in climatic melodrama. Seeing a familiar tan corduroy and a quilted down coat, she flung herself into the soft fabrics. Joe and Tony returned the embrace; Joliana was so grateful that both her father and husband had not been hurt. Breaking the bear hug, they surveyed the scene around them. Where was everyone? No Hank. No Pete. No Bette. No Darcy. Joliana turned and caught Darcy just emerging from the cellar steps. Blood stains darkened her black coat, and splotches dotted her high angular cheeks, which were strained in anguish. With her right arm, she brushed away some annoying stray hairs that were sticking to her face. "They're all dead," was all she said. With her left hand, she flung something shiny at Joliana. "That belongs to you. Bette doesn't need it anymore."

Joliana hastily caught her treasured charm bracelet and shoved it into her coat pocket. She rushed back into the basement, commanding that she not be followed, that she go alone. Everyone drew in a deep breath and waited. She returned, looking like Darcy, christened in the crimson tide, but also accompanied by an unexpected neighbor. Geraldine. Joliana had found the lights on and the older woman wandering about the basement. They had exchanged mute glances that spoke of the awful calamity that had happened here.

Hank was dead.

Bette was seriously injured.

Pete had disappeared.

And there was no trace of any leather case or Smith & Wesson gun.

Joliana reached the lower end of Windslow Street, her heart sending its drum beats to her ears. This was where it had all happened, on this seemingly innocent street. How could such mischief and malevolence happen behind these sturdy clapboards and white picket fences? Everything looked so peaceful. Even Mille, who sat on the discolored bench where Windslow Street began, seemed to have her ship even-keeled. Well, maybe not. As Joliana nodded to Mille, she noticed that the slender woman still dressed like Mary Poppins in plaids and stripes and bright colors, which were discordant with her heavy, mud-soaked boots. But this lady didn't fly; instead, she rode her trusty one-speed bike and somehow managed her floor-length calico. Mille liked to munch, and today was no exception as she jammed cold, boiled eggs and toast into her mouth.

Joliana hastened her pace a bit; she really didn't want to chat with Mille, who, at times, was more contentious than Geraldine and Lizzie put together. Hank's house was now within view. The bungalow looked so sad; it ached for a paintbrush and a fresh wash of color. But it also seemed to be grieving. And rightly so. Only last week had the last of the yellow police tape blown away. The house now stood alone and empty. Hank would never return since Pete's aim had accurately made its mark. So the property all went to his niece, Darcy. The newspaper had detailed this situation, stating that a holographic will had been found in the house, scribbled and stained with what looked like coffee, but intelligible. It had been a fortuitous find, since the police had swarmed the place, seeking clues for the murders and the long-ago bank robbery. The authorities had wanted to tie up this case in a nice brown parcel but couldn't. The papers were sketchy in detail, talking in journalist circles. But Joliana was pretty sure about some things. Hank was dead, by Pete's own hand, but Pete was long gone, the bank money in his possession. His disappearance was so quick, like a vapor that had been absorbed into the sky. But not so. Joliana smirked and wiped sweat from her forehead. She believed he had had an accomplice, someone who was waiting and ready to zoom him off. Jerry. Lizzie had actually started this town rumor, but she was certain that this was true. Jerry and his old cruiser were missing, and she had discovered discarded foil candy wrappings in front of Hank's house that infamous day.

Joliana stood and gazed at the badly peeling house. Sad, sad memories. While Darcy would one day complete her prison stay and return to this homestead, Darcy's friend and Joliana's twin sister, Bette, would not. Hank had clumsily fired his gun, hoping to down Pete, but instead hit Bette. Bette had not died right then but had remained in critical condition at City Hospital for several days. Her twin had not regained consciousness, but Joliana had sat and spoke with her, attempting to connect with this dying woman. Joliana fingered the charm bracelet, which playfully glistened in the sun, feeling a connection with her sister. She had wanted to know more about her past and hounded her father for information. But stubborn Joe only threw up his hands and declared ignorance. Since the simple funeral, Joliana had been working her own search, which was only in the baby-step stage.

Joliana continued down Windslow Street. Geraldine's house. The elegant gray house, resplendent with white filigree and a pronounced widow's peak, stood very stately in the neighborhood. She squinted towards the pinnacle, the high noon sun bright in the sky. She could make out the beehive bun that Geraldine favored and the movements of an ovular object, which were probably her binoculars. Some things hadn't changed, but so much had. Geraldine and Lizzie were now housemates. Since Lizzie's house was declared inhabitable, she had sold the property and built an addition in the back of Geraldine's home for all her newly found treasures. Geraldine was now a part-time snoop. The rest of the day, she worked for the recently opened Marty's Complete, which combined all three of the marts in a central location. She was the new bookkeeper. It was a good fit for her; Geraldine could leave her house and resume some productivity, and the Williard family could count on her.

"Hm ..." Joliana looked over at Lizzie's once-charred lot, which had been rebuilt overnight. A mustard-colored Colonial stood in its place. It boasted reduced-sized glass panes that matched the decorum of the street, except that it looked to be right off the assembly line. However, the front yard was not perfect, with its muddy lumps and odd rock piles. She heard voices, but they were not coming from this new house but a little ways down. It was Tony and Dad, as well as Boomer, who was romping and frolicking about. The two of them were joking and roasting each other in good fun. That was the something good that had come from this situation: her father and husband were now comrades. They would often ride together to the mart or just around town, stopping here and there for a burger. And even though her father had refused to assist her in her search for the past, he had helped them in the present. Remarkably, Joe had opened his purse strings to money Joliana never knew existed. He distributed even amounts to the children for future college tuition. To her, he had gifted enough to fully cover the costs of any selected schooling, although he strongly encouraged nursing. In his opinion, he believed that Joliana's earlier nursing training had saved his life, as well as Geraldine's. So she had resumed her life behind the desk with thick, leaden textbooks; however, not with the intention of nursing but with a direction for social work. She wanted to better figure out all these people who surrounded her.

Joliana heard other voices. This time, she could not place who they were. They came from Lizzie's old homestead. Her curiosity had been baited, and she turned and sauntered back up the street. A woman stepped from a pink Cadillac, puffing so hard on her cigarette that the smoke encircled her like a mini forest fire. She wore a satin ebony gown, with white gloves that went to her elbows. The woman motioned for the remaining passengers to leave the car. Out came a teenage boy with purple hair, holding two small animals that appeared to be ferrets. A younger girl, perhaps his sister, followed, and she was dressed in a sequined-covered dance costume with flesh-colored tights. The girl was singing and performing pirouettes in the muddy yard, oblivious to ruination of her lovely outfit. Another boy emerged, a bit older than the other. He wore huge glasses, which didn't seem to help as he stumbled on the gravel and twigs with his armload of books. Then came the father, or who could perhaps be the father. He was exceptionally thin, his bony knees accented by the khaki shorts and white ankle socks. His graying hair looked like a perm gone bad, with curls and frizz emanating from his head. The woman in black was shouting directions at him, and he nodded obediently as he lifted carton after carton of goods, which were well over his weight. The bizarre family made a queue to the house and slammed the oaken door.

Joliana moved in a bit closer. Should she or shouldn't she? She could be the self-designated welcome wagon. She could rush home and bake up a nice orange cranberry bread and present it to them. Perhaps she could get her children to volunteer in cleaning up their front yard. Or maybe she should just mind her own business. Resolutely, she stood at the newly matted doorstep that, for some odd reason, said "Keep Out" in bold, black lettering. She lifted up the solid brass knocker and let it fall.

About The Author

The author, J. A. Elaine, was raised in Wethersfield, Connecticut; however, she currently lives in the New Haven County with her husband and four children. She is employed as a licensed professional counselor in an area college. Other interests include watercolor painting, calligraphy, singing, and, of course, reading, This is her first book.

CPSIA information can be obtained at www.ICGtesting.com
Printed in the USA
BVOW031158080413

317592BV00001B/5/P